SWIM TEAM

1

SWIMMERS, TAKE YOUR MARKS!

Other Avon Camelot Books in the
SWIM TEAM *Series*
by Janet E. Gill

#2: FLY 'N' FREE

Coming Soon

#3: FOUR'S A TEAM

Avon Books are available at special quantity discounts for bulk purchases for sales promotions, premiums, fund raising or educational use. Special books, or book excerpts, can also be created to fit specific needs.

For details write or telephone the office of the Director of Special Markets, Avon Books, Dept. FP, 1350 Avenue of the Americas, New York, New York 10019, 1-800-238-0658.

SWIM TEAM

1

SWIMMERS, TAKE YOUR MARKS!

JANET E. GILL

This is a work of fiction. Names, characters, places, and incidents either are the product of the author's imagination or are used fictitiously. Any resemblance to actual events, locales, organizations, or persons, living or dead, is entirely coincidental and beyond the intent of either the author or the publisher.

AVON BOOKS
A division of
The Hearst Corporation
1350 Avenue of the Americas
New York, New York 10019

Published by arrangement with the author
Visit our website at **http://AvonBooks.com**
Library of Congress Catalog Card Number: 96-95129
ISBN: 0-380-78672-9
RL: 4.6

First Avon Camelot Printing: June 1997

CAMELOT TRADEMARK REG. U.S. PAT. OFF. AND IN OTHER COUNTRIES, MARCA REGISTRADA, HECHO EN U.S.A.

Printed in the U.S.A.

OPM 10 9 8 7 6 5 4 3 2 1

For Carole, my swimmer

one

Tammy Tallman followed her mom and grandmother into the entry of the small, white church. Behind them, the door clicked closed, shutting out the bright April sun. Tammy's breath caught a sweet floral scent. It came from the pink carnations and white and lavender roses that filled the huge vase by the doorway to the sanctuary.

Tammy rushed to look through the door. Bouquets with more of the same flowers stood on both sides of the altar. Along the ends of the pews ran twined blue and lavender ribbons. A sky-blue candle stood in a holder on each pew.

''It looks beautiful,'' Tammy said to her mom and grandmother, who'd joined her.

Oma, the name Tammy called her grandmother, stroked Tammy's long, light brown hair. ''Your mother will have a fine wedding.''

Tammy didn't want to think about that part. For her, there was only one good thing about the day. ''Can I get dressed now?'' she asked.

Her mom checked her watch. ''Sure. Melissa and

Chuck should be here soon. The dresses are upstairs in the first dressing room. Do you want some help?''

''Mom, I'm in fifth grade. I think I can dress myself.''

Her mom grabbed Tammy's hands. ''Are your hands clean?''

''Mom,'' Tammy said, yanking them away.

Oma chuckled. ''You grow so fast, we forget, *Liebchen.*''

Oma and her family had moved to the United States from Germany when she was a girl. She still used some German words. Tammy liked to be called *liebchen.* It meant something like ''loved one'' or ''sweetheart.'' Hugging her grandmother, Tammy rubbed her cheek against the silky fabric of Oma's gray, flowered dress.

Oma gave Tammy and her mom a small push. ''Get upstairs and change. Guests will be arriving soon.''

Tammy took the stairs two at a time, not waiting for her mom. At the top, she headed for the first dressing room. Tap, tap, tap went her new shoes on the hall's hardwood floor. She gazed down. Light from the window at the end of the hall gleamed off the patent leather. She smiled in excitement and opened the dressing room door.

Locking it behind her, she gazed around the small room. To her left stood a low chest and a full-length mirror. A clothes rack against the far wall held two bridesmaids' dresses. A blue one for her. Lavender for Melissa.

''Oh,'' Tammy breathed, looking at them. She'd barely slept all night thinking about this moment.

She crossed the room and held out the long skirt. ''The blue of an April sky,'' her mother had said when

they chose the fabric. Tammy glanced out the windo[illegible]
Her mom was right.

The bodice was shirred. Long sleeves puffed almost to the elbow, then were tight to the wrist. Tammy recalled picking this dress out. She, her mom, and Melissa, Tammy's thirteen-year-old sister, had gone to a seamstress to choose a pattern for the bridesmaids' dresses. When the seamstress showed Tammy a picture of this dress, she knew it was the dress she wanted. Once, in a storybook, she'd seen one just like it. A princess had been wearing it.

Tammy hadn't expected Melissa to agree. They rarely agreed on anything. But Melissa liked the style. Tammy wondered if Melissa had read that book, too.

Tammy slipped out of her shoes, then took off her sweatshirt and jeans. The cool air raised goose bumps on her arms. Two other hangers held long half slips. She put hers on, then the dress. Lifting the skirt, she slipped her shoes on. Two circlets of pink roses lay on the chest. Choosing one, she turned to the full-length mirror.

"Oh," she said again as she stared at her reflection. She smoothed her hair, then slowly lowered the flowers onto her head.

Suddenly, in her mind, she stood on a platform in a great hall. Below her clustered men and women dressed in fabulous clothing. Furs. Brocades. Velvets and lace. Beside her, a handsome man raised a golden crown.

"I crown you Princess Tammy," he said, and set it in place.

"Princess Tammy, Your Royal Highness, the most

...cess in the land,” everyone said together.
...owed. The women curtsied.
...y, let me in!”
...my jumped at the words. The royal gathering
...ned.
...In a second, Melissa,” she said in her best princess voice.

The door rattled. “Right now! I have to hurry. People are starting to come.”

Tammy peered through the window. Three cars sat in the gravel parking lot. A man and woman walked toward the church.

The door rattled again. Tammy took one last look in the mirror. “Princess Tammy,” she mouthed. Smiling, she floated to the door.

“Tammy!” Melissa began as the door opened, then stopped and stared. “Tammy,” she said, her voice softer now, “you look fantastic. That dress is the same color as your eyes.”

Tammy stared back at her sister, surprised. She never said nice things like that. Eyes the color of an April sky. A small shiver of pleasure went through Tammy.

The moment passed as Melissa barged into the room. She stripped out of her T-shirt and jeans, kicked off her tennis shoes, and reached for her slip.

“Are your hands clean?” Tammy asked.

Melissa stopped and looked at her hands. “Of course they’re clean. What kind of stupid question is that?”

While Melissa dressed, Tammy hovered, fluffing out the long skirt, straightening the sleeves.

Melissa opened a shoebox she’d carried in. She slid on patent-leather flats, then moved to the mirror. Tammy held the circlet to set on Melissa's dark hair. Almost as tall as Melissa, Tammy reached up slightly, then stopped.

"What's that around your neck?"

Melissa fingered the pearl hanging from a fine gold chain. "Chuck gave this to me. To wear today. He . . ."

Tammy shoved the circlet into Melissa's hand and turned her back. Melissa punched Tammy's arm.

"He has one for you, too. He'll bring it as soon as he gets everything settled downstairs."

"I don't want one," Tammy said.

"You have to wear it. Mom said so."

Just as Tammy expected. Chuck bought the necklaces because of their mom, not for Tammy and Melissa.

"It's her wedding, after all," Melissa went on.

"Don't remind me," Tammy said.

Melissa grabbed Tammy's arms and spun her around. "Chuck is a really great guy. He loves Mom and she loves him. I don't know what your problem is, but if you spoil today . . ."

A knock interrupted Tammy's answer. When Melissa answered it, Oma and their mom entered the room. Their mother wore a pale pink silk dress and patent leather pumps. Her pearl necklace gleamed softly.

"You look really pretty, Mom," Melissa said.

Their mother's cheeks flushed as she touched the pearls. Tammy didn't have to ask where they came from. Chuck, of course.

"*Ach,*" Oma said, "look at you two girls. You look *wunderbar!*"

Wunderbar, Tammy knew, meant "wonderful" in

German. Almost sounded like it, too. Except the way Oma said the word, it seemed as if it started with a *v*.

"I wish your father could be here to see you two," Tammy's mother said. Her eyes were shiny.

Their father had died when Tammy was four. Sometimes it seemed to Tammy that she remembered him. Still, she knew most of her memories were from stories told by her mom and Melissa.

"If he were, we wouldn't be doing this," Melissa said.

Their mom gave a quick laugh. "I guess not. My head is so filled up with thoughts and memories, I'm not thinking straight."

Oma put an arm around her daughter's shoulder and squeezed, then handed Tammy a small, blue velvet-covered box. "This is from Chuck. I wouldn't allow him upstairs. It's bad luck for a groom to see his bride before the ceremony."

Tammy opened it. A necklace like Melissa's. She wished it weren't so pretty. She didn't want to like it. The sound of organ music rose from downstairs as Oma fastened the chain around Tammy's neck. Pulling a comb from her pocket, Oma ran it through Tammy's hair, then Melissa's.

"Our bouquets are in the other dressing room," their mother said. She carefully hugged both girls. "The start of a whole new wonderful life," she whispered.

Tammy shut her mind to the words.

two

Tammy, Melissa, their mother, and Oma waited outside the sanctuary. From inside came the murmur of conversation combined with organ music. Tammy sniffed her bouquet of pink roses and white baby's breath. A blue ribbon that matched her dress trailed from the flowers. The organ music grew louder.

"Time," Oma whispered.

Tammy was to go down the aisle first, then Melissa. Opa, Tammy's grandfather, had died two years ago. Oma would walk with Tammy's mother. Tammy looked down the aisle. At last night's practice, it had seemed short. Now, it stretched on forever.

At the end stood Chuck, tall, fair-haired, dressed in a dark suit. He smiled at her with his special smile. It always invited her to smile back. Sometimes she did. Not this time. She had the long aisle and all those people watching to worry about. What if she tripped over her skirt and fell? The thought sent her heart rising to her throat.

Oma whispered in her ear. "You look like a princess, *Liebchen.*"

The crown settled on Tammy's head. She moved forward, step, pause, step, pause, to greet her subjects.

Following the ceremony and picture taking, everyone gathered downstairs for the reception. After about forty-five minutes, Tammy wished she could go home. She'd drunk all the punch she wanted, eaten all the tiny sandwiches, nuts, and mints she could hold. She'd had enough of people telling her how lucky she was to have such a fine new father. What was lucky about that? It meant she had to move from San Francisco to Seattle, where Chuck worked. Leave her friends, her school. Leave Oma.

Tammy helped herself to a second piece of wedding cake. Licking the sweet icing off her fingers, she sat in a chair in a corner. Chuck joined her there. He crouched to her level.

"You sure look nice," Tammy," he said. "That dress is the same color as your eyes."

"That's what everyone says."

"Guess I'll have to come up with something more original." His face grew serious. "How about your smile is like sunshine on a rainy day?"

Tammy frowned. "There isn't sunshine on a rainy day."

"I know. I haven't seen you smile since the pictures were taken."

Tammy took a bite of cake and chewed slowly.

"Tammy," he said, "I know we're making big changes in your life. And I'm not sure you really want me to be in it at all. But I feel like the luckiest person in the world to have married your mom. And you two girls are part of my luck. I know I'm not your real father, but I promise I'll do my best to take care of you. I want us to be a family. If something's bothering you, we should talk about it. Not right now, probably, but later."

Tammy didn't want to discuss this. Not now. Not later. Not ever. "Thanks for the necklace," she said.

Chuck sighed. "You're welcome, Tammy." He stood and went to stand by her mom.

Tammy wished she could believe him, but her mom had dated other guys before Chuck. They'd acted just as sincere and caring. When she was seven, one of them, Larry, brought a lot of presents for her and Melissa. He took them horseback riding and to movies and the county fair. She told him once she wished she could have a kitten. Their apartment didn't allow pets. He gave her a white stuffed toy cat with blue eyes. She named it Fluffy and took it everywhere.

One day, Larry stopped coming around. Her mom said things didn't work out between them. Tammy waited weeks for him to call her. He never did. That's when she realized her mother's friends were nice to her and Melissa only to get her mother to like them. She and Melissa really didn't matter. She'd thrown Fluffy in a trash can on the way to school. She told her mom she lost the cat.

"Tammy."

Tammy jumped at the word. She gazed up at her mother.

"Chuck tells me you're not happy, baby." She took Tammy's hand and stroked it. "What's bothering you?"

Why'd Chuck have to say anything to her? "My stomach doesn't feel so good," Tammy said.

Her mother glanced at the empty cake plate. "How many pieces?"

"Two. And I had a lot of mints and punch."

"Well, sit quietly for awhile. You'll feel better. But don't eat any more." Her mom checked her watch. "Chuck and I head for the airport pretty soon. Just think, next time I see you, we'll have a house with a room of your own and a yard. Remember how we used to dream about those things?"

"Can I get a kitten?" Tammy asked.

She smiled at Tammy. "Let's get settled first."

A couple of months before, Chuck and Tammy's mom had purchased a house in Seattle. A moving van was taking the furniture there. After a brief honeymoon in Vancouver, British Columbia, Chuck and her mom would get things unpacked. Tammy and Melissa would fly there in a week.

Her mom squeezed Tammy's hand. "I'm going to run up and change. You're sure you're all right?"

"Yeah, Mom."

Shortly after, Melissa joined Tammy. "How come you're sitting over here?"

"My stomach hurts." Tammy patted her stomach. It had started hurting right after she told her mother it did.

Melissa pulled a chair up beside Tammy's and sat down. "How many pieces of cake, little piggy?"

"Two. How many did you have?"

"Three," Melissa said.

"So who's the little piggy, Melissa?"

Melissa made snorting pig noises. They both laughed.

Oma walked up to them. "Your mom and Chuck will

be leaving pretty soon.'' She glanced around. ''Oh, look. Here they are now.''

Chuck and their mom had come into the reception room. They headed right for Tammy and Melissa. The girls stood.

''I'm going to miss you two,'' their mom said. As she hugged the girls, Tammy breathed deeply of her mom's perfume. The scent reminded her of the sweet peas they'd grown on their apartment balcony the year before.

Next, Chuck hugged Melissa, then turned to Tammy. She didn't put her arms out. He patted her shoulder. ''We'll see you in a week.''

Everyone followed them upstairs and out on the porch, where their mom threw her bouquet. Then, in a flurry of rice, she and Chuck ran to their car. Someone had taped a big Just Married sign to the trunk.

Tammy, Melissa, and Oma waved until the car drove out of sight. Then Oma said, ''Are you girls hungry?''

They both groaned and shook their heads no. ''How about we rent a couple of movies?'' she asked. ''If you want to eat later, we'll order pizza.''

Tammy and Melissa grinned at each other. ''Great.''

Chuck and their mom had timed the wedding to fall during the school's spring break. Oma was taking them to San Diego for three days to see Sea World and the San Diego Zoo. They'd spend the rest of the week at Oma's apartment. Tammy really looked forward to that. The apartment building had an indoor pool. She loved to swim, and Oma always let her spend as much time in the pool as she wanted.

Heading upstairs to change, Tammy climbed the steps

slowly. In just one week, she would start a whole new life. She did love the idea of living in a house and having a bedroom all her own. Plus, she'd get to walk to school instead of taking a smelly old bus. And her mom had said she could have a kitten. Smiling with that thought, she skipped up the last three steps.

The next week flew by. For Tammy, the best part of the trip to San Diego was riding the elephant at the zoo. She sat high on the animal, swaying from side to side, as a man led it around in a large circle. She breathed the scent of hay and the elephant's dusty skin. She stroked it. It felt like the textured leather of one of her mom's purses.

While Tammy rode, Oma and Melissa waited behind the chain-link fence that walled off the riding area. When Oma called to Tammy, Tammy smiled and waved, and Oma took a Polaroid picture.

When the ride came to an end, the ticket taker handed Tammy a round sticker. On it were the words *I rode an elephant at the San Diego Zoo.* Tammy gave it to Oma to keep in her purse.

Tammy spent most of the rest of the week in the pool in Oma's building. Evenings, Oma checked Tammy's fingers, wrinkled from being in water all day. ''You'll be a raisin by the time you get to Seattle,'' Oma said, laughing

Finally, the week ended. Sunday morning, Tammy and Melissa boarded a plane for Seattle.

three

"Here we are," Tammy's mom said.

Under cloudy skies, she, Chuck, Tammy, and Melissa had driven from the airport to a new subdivision outside of Seattle. The name at the entry said Crestview. Some homes in the area were still being framed in. Others had curtains on thc windows and finished landscaping.

Chuck pulled the car into the driveway of a blue frame house with white trim. From the top story, two bay windows protruded. A low string fence kept foot traffic off the newly laid sod.

As the four climbed from the car, Tammy shivered in the coolness. She'd heard about rainy Seattle. She gazed up at the pale gray clouds. Did the sun ever come out here?

"Which one's my room?" Melissa asked, staring at the bay windows.

Tammy's mom pointed to the left-hand window. "Tammy's is on the right," she said.

Chuck took their suitcases from the car's trunk. By the time he reached the front porch, their mom had the door unlocked. Inside, the house smelled fresh, like new wood. They went into a small entry that led to the living room. The furniture from their San Francisco apartment had been arranged so the couch and chairs faced the brick fireplace.

"You didn't tell us it had a fireplace," Melissa said.

Chuck laughed. "Wanted to surprise you."

"Can we build a fire tonight?" Tammy asked. They'd never had a fireplace before.

"Sure," he said. "I'll get some wood."

From the living room, Tammy and Melissa hurried upstairs to see their rooms. Tammy's furniture had been moved in. The light blue rug complemented her blue curtains and quilted bedspread. Her bulletin board hung above her desk. She took the sticker from the San Diego Zoo from her jacket pocket and pinned it up. When she unpacked, she'd add the picture.

"I bought your school supplies," her mom told her. She gestured to a notebook, a package of pencils, and another of pink ballpoint pens on Tammy's desk. "You're all ready to start school tomorrow."

School. Tomorrow. The words lumped in Tammy's throat.

They went back downstairs and through the shiny new kitchen. Chuck led them out the back door onto a wide, low porch. "We'll get some outdoor furniture," he said. "A barbecue, too."

"Can I have friends over for barbecues?" Melissa asked.

"If you make any," Tammy said.

"Why wouldn't I?" Melissa glared at her.

"Girls, that's enough," their mom said. "Of course, Melissa will make friends. You, too, Tammy." She stroked Tammy's hair. "You'll do just fine."

Easy for you to say, Tammy thought.

A stained-wood fence ran around the backyard. New sod had been laid, leaving a wide, earthen swath by the fence.

"Can we plant sweet peas?" Tammy asked.

Tammy had liked growing sweet peas at the apartment. She'd placed vases of the sweet scented, pastel flowers around the apartment so she could smell them everywhere.

"Sure," her mom said. "We can put them by the apple tree." She gestured toward a tree in the far right corner of the yard. White flowers covered its branches.

"Apple tree?" Tammy said.

"It's one of the reasons we chose this house," Chuck told her. "All this land used to be a farm. This part was an apple orchard. The builders left some of the trees."

Tammy stared at the tree. "You mean apples will grow on that?"

Chuck nodded. "By September, those flowers will be apples."

"How?" Tammy asked.

"You city kids." Chuck laughed. "Wait and see."

As Tammy walked to the tree, the new sod felt springy under her feet. She gazed up into the branches. Bees flitted from one blossom to another. Listening, she heard their steady buzzing.

"I'm going to the store to get some wood for us to burn," Chuck said. "Anyone care to come? Tammy? Melissa?"

"I'll go," Melissa said. "I want to see the stores."

Melissa loved to shop. Tammy thought it was boring. "I want to unpack," she said.

"I'm going to call your grandmother and let her know you arrived safely," her mom said as they went into the house.

"All right," Chuck said. "Melissa and I will get the wood."

That evening, as Tammy prepared for bed, a knock sounded on her door. When she said, "Come in," Melissa entered. She flopped in Tammy's desk chair.

"I'm sorry for what I said about your making friends," Tammy said.

"Are you worried about it?"

"Aren't you?" Tammy asked.

"A little. But at my old school, we had a girl who moved there this year. She made friends real fast. I asked her how she did it."

"How did she?"

"She talked to everyone she was around. She said to say things that people like to hear or can agree with. Like 'Boy, last night's homework was hard.' Or something nice like 'I like your sweater. Where do you shop around here for cute clothes?' Don't talk about yourself unless people ask. And don't brag about things you've done or how much better your old school was."

Tammy thought a minute. "People want you to care about them before they care about you."

"Wow, Tammy, that's pretty smart. I guess that's just how it works."

Tammy climbed into bed. "Maybe I shouldn't wear my Sea World sweatshirt tomorrow. That might be like bragging I'd been there."

"Yeah," Melissa said. "Too bad. But you can wear

it next week.'' Sliding out Tammy's top drawer, she held up a blue-and-white striped sweater. ''Wear this. It looks really good on you.'' She put it back, then headed out of the room.

''Turn off the light, Melissa,'' Tammy said. When the door shut, she lay in the dark room whispering. ''Boy, last night's homework was hard. . . . I like your sweater. Where do you shop around here for cute clothes?''

four

Tammy and her mother paused at the entrance to the one-story brick school. A sign in front said Eastwood Elementary. Morning sunlight shone through broken clouds. It warmed Tammy's face as she peered in through the glass door.

"Ready, Tammy?" her mom asked.

Tammy swallowed. She wanted to say her stomach hurt and any minute she'd throw up. If that didn't happen, she would have a heart attack because her heart was beating so fast. Instead, she pulled the heavy glass door open. "Let's go."

In the wide entry, Tammy didn't see any other children, but school didn't start for half an hour. Her mom had brought her early to register. Chuck had taken Melissa to the junior high.

Tammy followed her mother to the office directly in front of them. To the right, a long hallway led to classrooms. The floor gleamed softly. Its pale tiles had the circles left by a waxing machine. An open door on the left showed a cafeteria/gym. The school smelled of wax and lunches and chalk dust.

In the office, a woman stood behind the counter. A

name plate said MRS. MUROSAKI. A row of open teachers' boxes lined one wall. A cluttered desk sat against another. In the third wall, a closed door bore the words PRINCIPAL'S OFFICE and under that, the name ROGER J. CLARK, all in black letters.

Mrs. Murosaki faced a blonde woman filling out a form. Beside her on the counter, a baby car seat held a tiny baby wrapped in a pink blanket. Tammy and her mom stepped forward, and Mrs. Murosaki moved down the counter toward them.

"I'd like to enroll my daughter in the fifth grade," Tammy's mom said.

Mrs. Murosaki set out a form and a pen. "My goodness, you're the second one this morning." She gestured to the other woman. "Are you from the Crestview development, too?"

When Tammy's mom nodded, Mrs. Murosaki said, "We've been enrolling a lot of kids from there. Our classes are pretty crowded right now. The good thing is that we'll have more room next year." She gestured out the back window where workers were framing up a building. The thud of a pounding hammer sounded faintly in the office. "You girls will have a brand-new classroom for sixth grade."

Tammy gazed around. Another girl sat in one of the chairs against the fourth wall. She wore jeans, a lightweight jacket, and an ash-gray sweatshirt. Her fingers twisted a strand of her long blonde hair. A boy about four or five years old stood beside her. His blonde hair was like a cap on his head.

"Sit down, Tammy," her mom said. "This will take a few minutes."

Choosing a seat three chairs from the other girl, Tammy settled her notebook and lunch bag in her lap. She stared straight ahead. *Say something to her,* she told herself. Trouble was, they hadn't had any homework yet to talk about. And if this girl was new, she wouldn't know the stores to shop in.

Something tugged Tammy's arm. She turned to see the small boy standing beside her.

"Did you just move here, too?" he asked.

When Tammy nodded, he said, "We live in Crest-view. We have a brand-new house."

"Me, too."

"Do you want to come see my house?"

"Ryan, leave her alone," the other girl said.

Tammy looked at her. "It's okay. I can't come now," she told Ryan. "I'm starting school."

"So is Lora." He pointed to the other girl. "She's my big sister. What's your name?"

"Tammy." She turned to Lora. "Are you in fifth grade, too?"

Lora moved down to sit beside her. A strand of hair was tied into a knot. "Yeah. I've never started a new school before. Have you?"

Tammy shook her head no. Lora reached into the small pack she carried and pulled out a rainbow-striped pencil. She held it out to Tammy.

"Thanks," Tammy said.

"I've got another one just like it," Lora said. "This way we're sort of like twins. Plus, we both live in Crest-view. Do you like to swim?"

"I love to," Tammy said.

"Are you on a swim team?"

''Swim team?''

''Yeah,'' Lora said. ''Where you swim almost every day all year. I was on one before we moved. I'm joining one here next fall.''

''I didn't know about swim teams,'' Tammy said.

''Maybe you can join, too. What's your best stroke?''

Tammy shrugged. She didn't have a *best* stroke. She did all of them about the same, which was not very well. ''I like to do butterfly,'' she said. She'd learned it that past summer in swim lessons.

Lora's eyes widened. ''Fly! That's a hard stroke.''

Tammy thought a moment. ''I guess that's why I like it.''

''Maybe we could hang out together today,'' Lora said. ''For lunch and recess?''

''Sure,'' Tammy said. Her chest swelled. She'd met a friend, and she hadn't even walked into the classroom.

She looked at the rainbow pencil. Reaching into the plastic pack in her notebook, she took out one of the pink pens her mom bought her. ''Now we have matching pens, too,'' she said, handing it to Lora.

Just then, Lora's mother joined them. ''You're all set, Lora,'' she said. She untied the knot in Lora's hair. ''Lora always does this when she's worried,'' she explained as she combed it smooth with her fingers. ''Your teacher's name is Mr. Henderson,'' she went on, then looked at Tammy. ''You're in fifth grade, too?''

''This is Tammy,'' Lora said. ''Tammy, this is my mom, Mrs. Davis.''

Tammy's mother stepped to them. Tammy introduced her.

"Looks like you two won't be alone on your first day," she said.

"Tammy lives in Crestview, too," Lora told her mom. "And she likes to swim."

"That'll be nice this summer," she said.

Before Tammy could ask what she meant, she went on, "And for now, you two can walk home together."

The baby, still on the counter, started fussing.

"That's Emily," Ryan said, going to her. "She's pretty new, but she can make a lot of noise."

"Two weeks old," Mrs. Davis said. "She made our move last week very interesting." Returning to the counter, she picked up the car seat.

"You sure you'll be all right?" Tammy's mom asked Tammy. "Want me to stay around awhile?"

"I'll be just fine, Mom." She wished her mother didn't always treat her like a baby.

"Okay. In that case, I'll go home and start job hunting. I'll pick you up after school."

"I know the way. I'll walk with Lora."

Her mom pursed her lips, then said, "Don't talk to strangers, and don't take a ride with anyone."

"We know," the girls said together.

They said good-bye to their mothers, then Mrs. Murosaki led them down the long hall to a classroom. Inside it looked almost like Tammy's schoolroom in San Francisco. Light came from a wall of windows across from them. In the front, a long blackboard had the cursive alphabet over it. Two bulletin boards displayed maps and pictures of South America. That was all right. Tammy had been studying South America at her old school. The teacher's desk, piled with books and papers, stood in the back corner by the windows.

The teacher was writing math problems on the blackboard. He wore gray slacks, a white shirt, and a red patterned tie. His dark hair touched his collar in back. He turned to them.

"I have two new students for you, Mr. Henderson." Mrs. Murosaki handed him the registration papers.

He frowned. "From Crestview, right?" he said. When she nodded, he continued. "I told them they needed to rush that new building through."

She didn't say anything.

"I'll need another table and chairs," he said.

"I'll have them brought in."

While they talked, Tammy studied Mr. Henderson. She didn't think he was glad to see her and Lora. When Mrs. Murosaki left, he thumbed through the registration papers.

"Who's Tammy?" he asked.

"I am," Tammy said.

He looked toward Lora. "And you're Lora?"

She nodded.

"Welcome to the class," he said, smiling now. "I don't want you to think I'm not glad you're here. It's just that I got two new students from Crestview right before spring break. This room is starting to bulge." He gestured at the rows of tables filling the center.

Tammy counted. Six rows, each with three tables. Eighteen tables. Two chairs at each one. Two times eighteen. She thought a moment. Thirty-six kids. She and Lora made it thirty-eight. Their table would be squeezed in almost to the back wall.

"You can see how crowded we are," he said. "We need that new addition right now." He set down the papers and returned to the blackboard. "Put your things in that closet in the back. I'll finish this and then get you your books."

"We're good students," Lora said, speaking for both of them. "You won't have to worry about us."

He turned, smiling. "My job is to worry about you. If you need help, be sure and ask."

They put away their jackets and lunches, then stood against the wall by the door, waiting for their table and chairs.

"He's nice," Lora whispered.

"I feel kind of guilty being here," Tammy told her. "Like we're taking up his time."

"Are you good in school?" Lora asked.

"Yeah, but what if I don't understand something?"

"Ask your mom or dad. Or sister or brother. Do you have any?"

"A big sister. But if I ask her, she'll just tell me I'm dumb or something."

Lora slipped her hand under Tammy's arm and squeezed. "Then ask me. We'll figure it out together."

Tammy smiled at her. Lora was going to be a good friend. Maybe she'd turn out to be the best friend Tammy had always hoped for.

School started in ten minutes, and gradually, other kids came into the room. They all stared at Tammy and Lora, but no one said anything.

Tammy remembered she wanted to ask Lora what her mother had meant earlier about swimming. Just then, though, a husky man carried a table and two chairs in.

He set them behind the last row. Mr. Henderson went to a cupboard on the side wall and took out several books. He gestured to Tammy and Lora. When they joined him, he gave books for social studies, English, and math.

"We have math first every day," he went on. "We're finishing up a unit on decimals. I hope you girls have worked on them."

"My class was doing that when I left," Lora said.

Decimals? Tammy thought. She didn't know anything about them. Her stomach started churning. She'd need help the first minute class started. She knew Mr. Henderson meant it when he said he would help her. Still she couldn't tell him. She'd seen his relieved look when Lora said she knew decimals.

five

Tammy and Lora carried the books and their notebooks to their table and put them in the storage drawers underneath. The bell rang. All the kids milling around quickly took their places. Mr. Henderson stepped before the class.

"Good morning and welcome back," he said. "I hope you all had a good spring break."

"You bet." "Yeah." Everyone was smiling.

"We have two new class members," he told them. "Please stand up, girls."

As Tammy and Lora rose, everyone turned to them. For a moment, to Tammy, the room seemed to be filled with nothing but pairs of staring eyes. Warmth rushed up her neck to her cheeks.

"Lora Davis is on the right," he said. "She's from Idaho. Tammy Tallman's from San Francisco. Please make them feel welcome today. Help them find their way around school."

He pulled out a green book and checked roll. Two chairs were empty. "Looks like Pete and Yvette are having an extra long vacation," he said.

"Yvette's got chicken pox," a girl told him.

He set the book on his desk, then asked them to stand for the Pledge of Allegiance. As they sat back down, he walked to the blackboard. "This week we're going to review decimals. This is our preliminary test—to tell me who's having trouble with what. We'll have our unit test on Friday."

Groans came from around the room.

"What am I hearing?" he said. "I thought for sure you'd spend your break studying for this."

"Sure, Mr. Henderson," a red-haired boy said. "Like you spent yours doing lesson plans."

Mr. Henderson laughed. "Of course, Tim. That's what teachers do." He tapped the blackboard. "Let's get started with these. Does anyone have any questions?" When no hands went up, he said, "Well, then, what are you waiting for?"

While he talked, Tammy studied the problems. One row each of five addition, five subtraction, five multiplication and five long division. Everything was okay except for the dots between the numbers. What did they mean?

Should I tell him I don't know this? Tammy thought. No. All the kids would think she was really dumb.

Notebooks clicked as paper was removed. Several kids lined up at the pencil sharpener near Tammy and Lora's table. As the machine chirred, the scent of wood drifted to Tammy. She took out a piece of paper and the rainbow pencil. Lora held hers, too.

"I've never done decimals before," Tammy whispered to Lora.

"Pretend it's money," Lora told her. "Like the first

problem—2.00 + 4.50 + 6.35—is really adding dollars and cents.''

''Oh,'' Tammy said. ''That's easy.'' She solved the first two rows and moved to the multiplication, 4.61 × .25. How did you multiply twenty-five cents by four dollars and sixty-one cents? That didn't make sense. She grinned slightly. Make sense? Or cents?

The room was quiet, the only sound the rubbing of erasers and Mr. Henderson's footsteps as he strolled around the desks. She multiplied the numbers and got the answer 11,525. But what to do with the little dot? She wrote

$$\begin{array}{r} 4.61 \\ \underline{\times .25} \\ 11525 \end{array}$$

That lined the dots up. She stuck one between the 5 and the two.

She glanced at Lora's paper. Lora was already working on division. Her answer for the problem Tammy had just done was 1.1525.

''The next problem was .69 – 2.3 = ?. She set her pencil down. She couldn't do these. She sat staring out the window until Mr. Henderson called time.

''Everyone stand up and stretch,'' Mr. Henderson said after the papers had been collected.

''I think my brain died over vacation,'' Tim said.

Mr. Henderson laid an ear on Tim's head. ''No, it's working. It's saying 'Give me a break.' Not a bad idea. Take three minutes.''

''I really failed that,'' Tammy said.

"I'll show you how to do them after school," Lora said.

Two girls approached the table. One was the girl who'd told about Yvette and the chicken pox earlier.

"Hi," she said. "I'm Mary White. And this is Kim Lee." She gestured to the girl beside her.

"Hi," Tammy and Lora said.

"How'd you like that test?" Mary made a face.

"It wasn't bad for me," Lora said, "but Tammy's never had decimals."

"Then you'll be in the slow group tomorrow," Mary said.

"The slow group?" Tammy said. This was even worse than she'd thought.

"Mr. Henderson calls it review group. It really makes you do better on the unit test. I've been in every one this year, and I always pass the final test. Don't worry. Mr. Henderson will help you."

"I'm going to show Tammy how to do decimals after school," Lora said.

"Oh, where do you live? Can I come?" Mary asked.

"Crestview," Tammy said.

Mary's face fell. "That's too far from my house. I take a bus to school."

"Do you guys play softball?" Kim asked.

"I do," Tammy said as Lora nodded.

"Good," Mary said. "Girls play the boys at lunch recess every day. Yvette's one of our best players, and since she's out for the week, we can use some help."

Mr. Henderson called the class back to order. Tammy watched Kim and Mary return to their desks. She was glad they'd come to talk to her and Lora and also glad Mary couldn't come home with them after school.

When social studies time came, the class went to the cafeteria/gym to learn a traditional dance of Bolivia. Lunch tables had been taken down, and everyone clustered in the center of the room. Mr. Henderson spread them out some, then demonstrated how to do the dance. Tammy made sure she stood next to Lora. Mary and Kim Lee squeezed in beside them.

They practiced first without music. The steps involved crossing one foot before another, then behind, then before, along with stamping. Mr. Henderson counted out the rhythm. Tammy concentrated on her feet, but she kept ending up after everyone else. Finally, he played the music.

Tammy tried to do the steps, but the more she thought about where her feet should be, the more confused she got. Her shoulders tensed; her face grew hot. She wished she were by the door so she could dance right out of the gym. Instead she stopped and let the dancers go on without her.

"Just relax," Lora told her. Lora's feet were moving fast with the rhythm. "Do what the music tells you. If you miss a step, it doesn't matter."

Tammy took Lora's hand and, while Lora danced, Tammy ran back and forth. That was better. Now, when the music said to stamp, Tammy did. Hard. So did the others. The room resounded. She stamped the next time, too. But then she followed the stamp by crossing her foot over, then behind, then over and stamped again.

"Hey, I did it," she said as she crossed a foot over.

Lora squeezed Tammy's hand.

At recess, the girls won the softball game. Lora hit a home run; Tammy, a triple. Tammy pitched part of the game and struck four boys out. On the way back to class at the end of recess, Lora said, "You're really good at sports, Tammy."

"You, too," Tammy said.

"Mostly I like to swim. I can't wait till May seventeenth."

Tammy looked at her.

"That's when the Crestview Swim Club opens," she said.

"Swim club?" Tammy said as they entered the classroom.

Lora's grin was wide. "Didn't your parents tell you about it? Everyone who owns a house in Crestview belongs. It's got a great outdoor pool."

"You mean we can go there in the summer and swim?"

Lora's eyes sparkled. "Plus, there's going to be a summer swim team. We can be on it. How old are you?"

Tammy sat at their table. "Eleven."

Lora sat, too. "Me, too. We'll swim together. Eleven and twelve-year-olds swim in the same age class."

"I'm not the greatest swimmer," Tammy said.

"Don't worry. My dad says being on swim team is the best way to learn. And if you like fly, the coach will be really happy. Most kids don't swim that."

Lora's excited face told Tammy how important swimming was to her. Well, if being Lora's friend meant swimming on the swim team, that's what Tammy would do. A small voice whispered a question inside her head. *No matter what my mom says,* she answered.

six

After school, Tammy and Lora started home. Filtered sunlight cast pale shadows before them on the sidewalk. In yards, daffodils and tulips bobbed in a small breeze. It brushed Tammy's face, bringing with it the scent of flowers.

"Want to see the swim club?" Lora asked.

"Sure," Tammy said. Lora sounded as eager to show her as Tammy was to see it.

They changed streets. The new one led them to an entrance to Crestview Tammy hadn't seen before. Immediately inside was a parking lot. Beside the driveway into it stood a sign that read CRESTVIEW SWIM CLUB. A green canopied pick-up truck was parked under a fir tree.

They crossed the asphalt and stopped at a chain-link fence with an open gate. Beyond this, to the left, was a long, low building. A man in white overalls stood on a ladder brushing dark stain onto the shingles. The breeze carried the sharp scent of the stain.

The structure had three doors spaced along it. A sign above one door said OFFICE. The other two had signs: BOYS' LOCKER ROOM and GIRLS' LOCKER ROOM. To the girls' right was an empty L-shaped swimming pool. Its blue-tiled bottom gleamed dully. A concrete area for sunbathing covered a wide area beyond the pool.

Lora pointed toward the right, past the pool. "They told my dad they're going to put up concrete bleachers over there. Beyond the pool. For people to sit and watch the meets and stuff.

"The part with the diving board is for lap swimming," Lora went on. "That's where we'll be for swim team."

Tammy stared at the long stretch of pool. "You mean we have to swim that far?" Her only swimming had been in Oma's small apartment pool.

"Sure. Some races you swim back and forth four times."

"Oh," Tammy said. *Oh, no* is what she thought.

Lora laughed. "Don't worry, Tammy. We have practice every day before we start the races, I think for a whole month. You'll be ready."

"Have you been swimming a long time?"

"I started on a team when I was five. Ryan starts this year."

"He's going to swim laps?" Tammy asked. He seemed so small compared to that big pool.

"Little kids just swim one length. They're not strong enough for more."

Under her jacket, Tammy flexed her arm muscles. Would she be strong enough to swim that whole distance? "What if I sink in the middle?"

Lora laughed. "Tammy, you worry too much. I'll help you. We'll have fun."

Tammy forced a smile. *It's like I'm living on a roller*

coaster, she thought, as they turned and started home. *Mom marrying Chuck, down. New house, up. Starting school, down. Meeting Lora, up. Decimals, down. Pool, up. Swim team, maybe up, maybe down, especially if Mom objects.*

"Besides swim team practice, let's come every day," Tammy said. That would be the fun part, hanging out at the pool.

"Sure," Lora agreed.

A raindrop struck Tammy's face. She gazed up at the thickening clouds. "We better get home fast before the rain really starts," she said. She grabbed Lora's hand. "Besides, if we run, we'll get in shape for swimming sooner."

Tammy's house turned out to be only three blocks from the pool. They reached the front door just as the rain began to fall hard. Inside, after shedding their jackets and notebooks, the girls headed for the kitchen. Melissa sat at the kitchen table, reading a teen magazine. She looked up when they entered.

"Who's that?" she asked, gazing at Lora.

"Lora, my friend from school," Tammy said. She hoped that making a friend the first day impressed Melissa.

"I have to call my mom and tell her where I am," Lora said. She went to the phone on the wall.

While Lora talked to her mother, Tammy got pop and a sack of chips out. "Where's Mom?" she asked Melissa.

"She went to some job interview in Seattle."

Lora joined them. "I'm supposed to stay here till it stops raining," she said.

Tammy looked out the window. The rain was coming straight down. ''That might be a while.''

''We can work on decimals,'' Lora said, opening her pop can.

Melissa made a face. ''Decimals. Yuk. I never get those dots in the right place.''

Tammy ate some chips. ''Guess what, Melissa.''

Melissa eyed her. ''Good or bad?''

''Crestview has a swim club with a great big pool. We can go every day.''

''A pool? Cute guys and everything?''

Tammy shrugged. ''Probably.''

Melissa flipped to a page in her magazine. ''Look. Swimsuits. I'm going to get a real killer one.''

Tammy studied the page. The suits were cute, but pretty skimpy. ''Mom won't . . . ,'' Tammy began.

''It's my body,'' Melissa said.

''I don't want to be here when you tell her that.''

Melissa's smile was small.

''There's a swim team, too,'' Tammy went on. ''We can join it. They have races every week.''

''Why would I want to do that?'' Melissa asked.

''It's fun,'' Lora told her. ''We go to other pools, meet kids from all over.''

Melissa tipped her head. ''What do I have to do to be on it?''

''Practice every day for a month,'' Tammy said. She licked salt from her fingers. ''Swim lots of laps.''

''Tammy, I'll go to the pool only to lie in the sun and hang out with my friends. Maybe jump in and cool off once in awhile. I'm not the swimming type. And maybe I won't be around when you tell Mom about swim club.''

''It'll be okay,'' Tammy said quickly. She didn't want Lora to think there'd be a problem.

''Hey, you guys have an apple tree.'' Lora was looking out the window.

Tammy gazed at the tree. The hard rain had stripped off a lot of blossoms. They lay on the grass, circling the tree like a white necklace. She hoped the bees had flown home before the rain started.

''We have apple trees on our ranch,'' Lora continued.

''Ranch?'' Melissa said. ''With cows and horses?''

Lora nodded. ''We moved here so my dad can go to the University.''

''What about the ranch?'' Tammy asked.

''My mom's brother's running it for us.''

''Will you move back when your dad's done with school?'' Tammy asked. Already, the thought of losing Lora hurt like a sharp pain.

Lora shrugged. ''I don't know. Dad's not into ranching as much as my mom's family.'' She finished her drink, then stood. ''The rain's slowing down. Let's do decimals before I have to go.''

They left Melissa studying the page with swimsuits.

Retrieving their books, they climbed the stairs to Tammy's room. Lora went right to the bulletin board. On it, Tammy had put up a bunch of pictures.

''Wow, Tammy,'' Lora said. ''That's you riding an elephant. Weren't you scared? It's so big.''

Tammy joined her. ''It was fun. I was way high up. It swayed back and forth.'' She copied the motion. ''Kings and queens in India ride them, you know.'' Part of the time riding it, she'd pretended to be an Indian princess. Maybe someday she'd tell Lora that.

Lora pointed to a picture of an upside-down roller coaster. "Are you on that?"

"And Melissa," Tammy said. They'd taken that ride that past summer.

"But you're upside down. Why didn't you fall out?"

"It was going real fast. My grandmother said some kind of force kept us in. The ride was kind of weird, but fun."

"Uhhh," Lora moaned.

Tammy looked at her. Her face was pale. "Roller coasters make me really sick," she said. "Even thinking about them. Dad took me once, and I threw up during the ride. All over me and my dad. What a mess!" She sat on the bed. "What if I'd been upside down?" She giggled. "Everyone below me would have gotten hit."

Picturing people running around screaming as throw-up flew through the air made Tammy giggle, too.

"Tammy," Lora said, "if you're brave enough to ride an elephant and that roller coaster, why are you worried about swim club?"

Tammy gazed at her hands, lying in her lap. Should she tell her? Would Lora laugh? "I guess I'm afraid I'll do something dumb," Tammy blurted out, "and people will make fun of me."

Lora put an arm around Tammy's shoulder.

"I won't let that happen," Lora told her.

The warmth of Lora's arm spread through Tammy.

seven

Lora and Tammy worked on decimals for the next forty-five minutes. They'd covered multiplication and begun division when the rain finally stopped.

Lora stood and stretched. "I need to get home. I have to help my mom with dinner."

They packed up her books, then she and Tammy headed downstairs.

"You really learned fast," Lora said.

"You're a good teacher."

Lora beamed. "That's what I'm going to be when I grow up."

"Really?" Tammy said. She'd never thought much about what she wanted to do someday. Now, she wished she had plans for the future, too.

"I like showing how to do things," Lora went on. "I like to help people."

"You sure helped me. I wish I learned all the decimal stuff today. Then I wouldn't have to be in the slow group."

"Ask your mom or dad to explain division tonight," Lora suggested.

"My dad died when I was four," Tammy told her.

"Oh, Tammy." Lora's expression was sad. "That's too bad."

"It's okay," Tammy said quickly. "I don't remember him very well. My mom just married Chuck. He's from here. That's why we moved."

"Then ask him," Lora said. She pulled on her jacket and picked up her books.

"Maybe." Tammy didn't think Lora would understand why she didn't want to.

Tammy walked outside with Lora. The cool air felt damp.

"Where do you live?" Tammy asked.

"Just a couple of blocks away. Dad drove me around a lot last week, so I'd know where things are. I remember that rack of mailboxes down there." She pointed to a covered wood stand holding mailboxes. One of the boxes looked like a miniature red barn.

"See you tomorrow," Lora said. She waved and walked off.

Tammy returned to the kitchen. Melissa was taking plates from the cupboard.

"Mom called," she said. "Chuck's bringing Chinese take-out for dinner. She wants us to set the table."

"I hope he remembers I like barbecued pork," Tammy said.

Melissa handed Tammy the plates. "Don't worry, Tammy. He knows you always get that."

"I think you should join swim club with me," Tammy said as she set plates around the table. "You know how Mom is. If I ask to do it by myself, she'll get all upset—like I'm going to drown or something. She might agree if you go, too." Tammy set the last plate down. ‘‘Maybe you could tell her you’re joining. After she says we can, you could change your mind.’’

‘‘Then she’d be mad at me.’’

Tammy traced the rim of a plate with her finger. ‘‘I could just not tell her I signed up.’’

‘‘How would you keep her from finding out?’’

Tammy sighed. ‘‘Melissa, I have to do this.’’

Melissa put a handful of silverware on the table. ‘‘Okay. Tell her at dinner. If she makes a fuss, I’ll help you out.’’

Tammy took a deep breath. ‘‘Thanks, Melissa.’’ She looked at the silverware. ‘‘Aren’t we using chopsticks?’’

Melissa giggled. ‘‘I’m being safe. Remember last time we had Chinese?’’

Tammy thought back to when Chuck brought them Chinese take-out in San Francisco. He’d decided they should learn to eat with chopsticks, and he banned silverware from the table. By the time they finished dinner, noodles, rice, and vegetables littered the floor and their laps. They’d ended up getting out forks to finish the meal, and a broom and wet cloth to clean up.

‘‘I’m going to try chopsticks again if he brings them,’’ Tammy said. ‘‘But leave a fork by my place, just in case.’’

Their mother arrived home shortly. A few minutes later, Chuck came in. He set a large, white bag on the table. He removed boxes of food from the sack, lining them up in the middle of the table. The tangy aromas wafting from them made Tammy’s mouth water. Each box had Chinese writing on top. She wished she knew what the symbols for barbecued pork looked like.

Finally, from the sack, he pulled a small box. "Last but not least."

She took it. "Barbecued pork! Yum." She sat at her place.

Her mom, Melissa, and Chuck joined her at the table.

"Told you, Tammy," Melissa said. "Tammy thought you'd forget the pork," she told Chuck.

"Not a chance." Chuck winked at her mom as he passed Tammy a small bag. "I even remembered the hot mustard and sesame-seed packets."

"And the chopsticks?" She motioned to the floor by her chair. She'd covered it with dish towels.

He laughed. "Better safe than sorry," he said and handed her a pair of chopsticks wrapped in paper.

His smile made her want to smile back. She didn't. His wink at her mom had told Tammy he brought the barbecued pork to please her mom. He knew Tammy would be upset if he hadn't gotten it. That, in turn, would have upset her mother. Thinking about it, Tammy's worry about joining the team increased. He'd side with her mom.

Tammy shook out the thin-sliced pork onto her plate. She tore open the mustard and sesame-seed packets. Emptying them beside the pork, she dipped a piece in each. She loved the spicy taste of the mustard—the way it tingled her tongue and made her eyes water.

Melissa, Chuck, and her mom were talking about Melissa's first day. At least, Melissa was talking—about teachers who gave tons of homework and a girl from Crestview she'd liked.

"How'd your day go?" Chuck asked Tammy when Melissa took a breath.

"Yes, Tammy," her mom said. "Did you enjoy that girl—what was her name?"

"Lora," Tammy said. "She came over after school. On the way home, she showed me the Crestview Swim Club."

"Oh, no, that was supposed to be a surprise," Chuck said. "I was going to take you two by tonight. How did you like it?"

"The pool's great." Tammy took a deep breath. She might as well jump right in. Jump right in. *Good one, Tammy,* she thought. "Lora said there's going to be a summer swim team. She wants me to join with her."

"What does a swim team do?" her mom asked.

"We practice and then race against other swim teams."

Her mother frowned. "You're not a very strong swimmer, Tammy. How could you race?"

Tammy couldn't admit that was her worry, too. She smiled, hoping her expression made her look confident. "Lora's dad says being on a swim team is the best way to learn to swim. Her little brother's joining."

"That little boy?" Tammy could tell by the tone of voice her mom was wondering about Lora's parents' sense of responsibility. "I don't . . . ," she began.

Tammy's heart sank. She looked toward Melissa. She was fiddling with her chopsticks and gazing everywhere but at Tammy.

"I think it's a good idea," Chuck said.

Tammy stared at him, openmouthed.

Her mother stared at him also, her mouth set. She gestured outside. Rain had begun again. "It rains all the time," she said. "She'll have a cold all summer."

"No, no," Chuck argued. "The sun shines a lot in the summer." Before she could say more, he went on. "There are a lot of lakes in this area, plus Puget Sound. These girls will have plenty of chances for water activities as they grow up. They need to be strong swimmers."

Now, Melissa stared at him. "Not me. I'm like a cat. I drink water. I don't swim in it."

"I'll tell you what," Chuck said to her. "I'll give you a swimming test. If you can pass it, you don't have to join swim team. If not, a summer of swimming will be good for you."

Melissa glared at Tammy. "Thanks a bunch."

Tammy looked toward her mom. She didn't look happy at all. Tammy didn't care. She felt like fireworks were going off inside her. Why Chuck stood up for her, she didn't know. But for the first time, she felt glad he was around.

"We'll try it," her mom said slowly, "but . . ."

"Don't worry, Mom," Tammy told her. "Lora's going to help me so nothing will go wrong." She dished up some rice and sweet-and-sour pork, then unwrapped her chopsticks. With them, she picked up a piece of pineapple. She got it in her mouth without dropping it. She lifted a piece of green pepper. *This is the best day of my life,* she thought.

An image of the pool rose in her head. Maybe she shouldn't be celebrating so soon. What if her mother changed her mind when she learned some races were four laps long?

* * *

Later that evening, Melissa came into Tammy's room. Tammy was lying on her bed, reading.

"You must be feeling good," Melissa said. Tammy could hear the anger in Melissa's voice. "You got your way, but you sure made a big problem for me."

Tammy sat up. "I'm sorry. But all you have to do is pass a test, just like we did when we took swim lessons."

"I'm afraid Chuck will make it harder than that. I don't know if I can swim well enough to please him."

"You can practice with Lora and me when the pool opens," Tammy told her. "Swim team doesn't start workouts until June first. Chuck won't test you till then."

Melissa sighed. "Practicing swimming with my little sister is not the way I want to spend my time at the pool." Melissa turned to leave. "Well, one thing you know now, Chuck is on your side."

"I just don't know why," Tammy said.

"Oh, Tammy, you're so dumb!" Melissa said. She slammed the door on her way out.

eight

Tammy arrived at school a little early the next morning. She found Mr. Henderson in the classroom.

"Good morning, Tammy," he said as she walked in.

"Mr. Henderson," she said, "I learned how to do decimals last night. I don't need to be in the slow group today."

He frowned. "Slow group?"

"The group to review decimals. That's what everyone calls it. Lora showed me about multiplying them yesterday. After school today, she's teaching me division."

"Oh, our review group," he said. "Tammy, that group has nothing to do with being slow. We work on the problems kids are having trouble with."

She handed him a paper covered with the decimal problems she and Lora had worked on.

He scanned the paper, then wrote three multiplication problems, each with decimals. "Solve these," he said, handing her the chalk. "If you get them right, you can skip the review group." He gave a short laugh. "Slow group. Guess I better have a talk with the class."

Tammy set her jacket and books on a front table, then worked the problems. She kept her hands out of his sight when she counted on her fingers. By the time she set the chalk down, most of the other kids had come in.

Mr. Henderson checked her answers. "Well done," he said. "Why don't you have Lora help you with division while I hold the review group?" He handed her a worksheet with math problems on it. "Practice on this tonight."

"Thanks, Mr. Henderson," Tammy said, taking the paper. "You can test me tomorrow on division."

"Our next unit will be on fractions," he said.

Tammy smiled. "Good. I already did those."

She carried her things back to her table. Lora was waiting for her.

"I get to work with you on division today instead of being in the slow group," Tammy told her.

"Good job," Lora said.

"We do fractions next," Tammy said. "Have you studied them?"

When Lora shook her head no, Tammy grinned. "Then it's my turn to help you."

Over the next weeks, at school, Tammy's class finished decimals and started fractions. They left South America and moved on to Africa. Mary and one other girl came down with chicken pox. The girls and boys continued to play softball at noon recess. The girls won several of their games because of Tammy and Lora's play.

One day, Lora said Tammy was a natural athlete.

"What's that mean?" Tammy asked.

"Just that sports come pretty easy to you. Look how

good you are in softball. I bet you won't have any trouble swimming.''

The words cheered Tammy.

Tammy thought about swim team every day. During the month's wait, she didn't mention it at home, for two reasons. Melissa had told her she should thank Chuck for standing up for her. Since she didn't believe he really did it for her sake, she didn't want to do that. She also didn't want to take a chance on her mother changing her mind. Especially since lately, her mom seemed always in a bad mood because she hadn't found a job yet.

Each night before Tammy went to bed, she crossed out the just-finished day on her calendar. Then she counted how many days until May seventeenth and the opening of Crestview Swim Club.

On the Saturday when fourteen days were left, Lora spent the night at Tammy's. They planted sweet peas along the fence, near the apple tree.

Tammy and Lora sat on the grass patting dirt over the seeds. Looking up into the tree, Tammy saw tiny green nubbins where the blossoms had fallen off. Little baby apples, she thought. Like magic.

''You know,'' she said to Lora, ''if a magician held a white blossom and blew on it and the petals flew away,'' Tammy held out her hand and blew, ''and then an apple appeared in his hand, everyone would say, 'Oh, wow, how did you do that?' This tree did the same thing, and no one even asks.''

Lora jumped up. She threw her arms around the large tree trunk. ''Oh, wow, Mr. Magic Tree,'' she said, ''how did you do that?''

Giggling, Tammy joined her. They stared up into the tree's thick branches. ''Lora,'' she said, ''don't you know magicians never tell their secrets?''

Later, as they prepared for bed, Tammy opened her closet door.

''That's the most beautiful dress I've ever seen,'' Lora said, gazing at the bridesmaid's dress hanging there. She took the dress out and held it in front of her.

Tammy beamed. ''I wore it at my mom's wedding. I was a bridesmaid.''

''It's like a princess's dress,'' Lora said.

Tammy nodded, pleased that Lora knew that. She showed Lora the necklace.

''Wow, Tammy,'' Lora said. She handed the dress to Tammy. ''Put it on. I want to see what a real princess looks like.''

Excited to wear the dress again, Tammy quickly changed.

''I love this necklace,'' Lora said as she fastened it around Tammy's neck.

Tammy gazed into the mirror. The magic of the dress was still there. She turned to Lora.

''Princess Tammy,'' Lora said, kneeling before her.

Tammy smiled. ''For your devotion, I will allow you to spend the night in the royal bedchamber.''

''Am I supposed to kiss your skirt?'' Lora asked.

Tammy giggled at the image the words brought. She covered her mouth with her hand. Princesses weren't supposed to giggle. ''That won't be necessary,'' she said.

''Good,'' Lora said, ''because it's kind of dusty.''

Tammy giggled again. Lora joined her.

"Time for bed, girls," Tammy's mom called from downstairs.

"Back to the real world," Tammy said.

"Not really," Lora said. "As long as you have that dress, you can always be a princess."

The following weekend, Lora's family drove to Idaho. Saturday afternoon, Tammy went with Melissa, their mom, and Chuck for hamburgers and a game of miniature golf.

She wished Lora were there to play golf. *Funny,* she thought as she hit her golf ball through a whirling windmill, *before I knew Lora, I didn't miss her. Now, it's like I'm missing something when she's not around.*

Wednesday afternoon, as usual, the girls walked home by way of the pool. Three rows of concrete bleachers now stood parallel to the lap end of the pool.

Tammy saw someone standing in the office. "Look," she said, pointing to it.

"Maybe we can sign up for swim team," Lora said.

They rushed to the office. Inside, a gray-haired woman stood behind the counter, pinning papers to a bulletin board. She looked at the girls.

"Can we sign up for swim team?" Tammy asked.

The woman smiled. "Do you live in Crestview?"

They nodded.

"I'm Lora Davis," Lora said. "She's Tammy Tallman."

"Glad to meet you. I'm Ms. Carter, the manager. We're starting sign-ups Saturday when the pool opens. I need some kids to sit at a sign-up table for a couple hours that day. You two interested?"

"Sure," they said together.

"Want to do the first hour?"

When they nodded, she said, "Be here about ten to get set up." She smiled. "That way your names will be first in the book."

Tammy and Lora grinned at each other.

The evening of May sixteenth, at Melissa's prompting, Tammy's mom took her and Melissa shopping for bathing suits in a nearby mall. Tammy chose a blue suit. *The color of an April sky,* she thought as she tried it on. Melissa fussed for a two-piece bikini, but their mom held firm. Finally, Melissa settled for a suit that looked like a two-piece from the back but one piece from the front. Tammy was glad she decided on that one. Tammy didn't want to tell her her stomach poufed out in the bikini.

At home, Tammy laid her suit out on her desk top. She set her new blue-striped beach towel and her leather sandals beside the suit. Taking her calendar from the drawer, she crossed out the sixteenth. A large star marked the following square. She gave a big sigh. She'd thought tomorrow would never come. Now, it seemed like only yesterday she and Lora had first stared through the fence outside the swim club.

Saturday morning dawned bright and sunny. Tammy put on her bathing suit, sweatshirt, and shorts and went downstairs.

The kitchen gleamed with the day. At the table, Chuck and her mom sat in a shaft of sunlight, eating cereal. Tammy laid her hand where the sunlight lay across the counter. The surface felt warm against her palm. She glanced out the window. Most of the sweet peas were up. With their tiny leaves unfurled, the plants looked like little green soldiers standing at attention.

She checked the time. Eight-thirty. Ms. Carter had said to come at ten, but Tammy and Lora wanted to get there earlier.

"Where's Melissa?" Tammy asked.

Her mother laughed. "Where do you think?"

Tammy knew. Still in bed. What she didn't know was how Melissa could sleep on such an important day.

"I could go over to the pool now," Tammy said, "and see if I could help with anything."

"Breakfast first," her mother told her.

"Oh, Mom," Tammy said, though she knew arguing would do no good. She took a bowl from the cupboard, poured in cereal, and added milk. She ate quickly, not tasting the food. "Now I'm ready," she said as she finished.

Her mother sighed. "Okay, go. Just don't get in anyone's way."

Tammy called Lora to let her know she was leaving.

nine

A banner stretching across the chain-link fence at Crestview Swim Club announced Grand Opening Saturday. As Tammy arrived, a car pulled in, and Ms. Carter climbed out.

"Hi, Ms. Carter," Tammy called.

"Good morning," Ms. Carter said.

Just then, Lora arrived. She carried a pink towel and a small sack.

The girls rushed to join Ms. Carter. She was juggling an armload of papers while unlocking the chain-link gate. Tammy took the stack from her. Ms. Carter pushed the gate open wide.

"I'm glad you girls came so early," she said. "Workers finished up late last evening. They left a mess."

She gestured to the sunbathing area. Scraps of paper, wood, and nails lay scattered around white beach chairs and tables with purple-and-white striped umbrellas.

"All that stuff needs to be swept up," she said. "And the concession delivery is due . . . ," she checked her watch, ". . . in twenty-five minutes. Bob Baxter will be here soon to take care of it. I know he'd appreciate your help."

"Sure," Tammy and Lora said.

Ms. Carter took her papers from Tammy and went into the office. Tammy and Lora went to the girls' locker room. Entering, they stepped onto a blue, perforated rubber mat that covered the concrete floor. As Tammy looked around, she bounced on the balls of her feet. She felt as though she were standing on a sponge.

White-tiled open shower stalls ran along one wall. Four rows of metal lockers filled the center. Tammy set her towel in the closest one. Lora added her towel and the small sack. Tammy locked the door with her new combination lock. She gave Lora the combination to memorize.

They left the room and moved to the lap end of the pool. Lora put her hands together in a diving pose. "I want to jump in right now," she said.

Squinting in the sunlight that made the water sparkle, Tammy gazed at the other end. A long way off. She moved her arms in a swimming motion. Could she swim that far?

"Girls!" Ms. Carter shouted from the office door. She held up a push broom and dustpan.

Tammy ran to get it. She pushed litter before her as she returned to Lora. They took turns sweeping and dumping trash into the waste receptacle by the concession stand.

The concession truck and Bob Baxter arrived at the same time. By then, Tammy and Lora had swept the deck clean. They helped Mr. Baxter stock the shelves with cookies, crackers, candy bars, licorice whips, and bags of various kinds of chips.

Tammy glanced at the clock above the stand's doors.

Nine forty-five. People would be arriving soon. She jostled Lora's arm. "We better get our table set up."

They hauled two chairs and an umbrella table over by the chain link gate. Ms. Carter brought out a sign that read SWIM TEAM SIGN-UP. She gave them the book to write names in. Their own names went on tags they stuck to their shirts. While Tammy hung the sign in front of the table, Lora ran to the locker room. She returned with the small bag and a paper towel. She handed both to Tammy.

"Something special for the first day," Lora said.

From the bag, Tammy pulled a cupcake. White frosting covered the top. On it, Lora had made the shape of a fish with gold sugar sprinkles. Beneath it, in blue sprinkles was the letter "T."

Lora pointed at the fish. "That's Tammy the Fish."

Tammy grinned at Lora. Spreading the paper towel out on the table, Tammy broke the cupcake in two pieces. "Yum, chocolate, my favorite. Thanks." She took a bite of the half with Tammy the Fish.

"Mine, too," Lora said. "That's how I knew you'd like it." When she'd finished her share, she licked her fingers and handed Tammy the pen. "The first person to sign up for swim team will be a fast swimmer," Lora said.

"Really?" Tammy asked. "Is that true?"

"I kind of made it up," Lora said, "but it will be true. I promise." She pushed the book to Tammy.

Tammy opened it, and on the top line wrote her name, age, address and telephone number. She gave Lora back the pen. "The second person who signs will be a fast swimmer, too."

Lora laughed and signed the book.

A couple minutes later, a blue pickup truck drove into the parking lot. Three teenagers, two boys and a girl, climbed out. White paste covered their noses. Both boys wore baseball caps, swim trunks, and sweatshirts. One was tall and slender; the other, shorter and stocky. The girl had on a gold-flowered cotton shirt over a gold bathing suit. Her nose was white, too. The black hair around her face had been braided into corn rows with bright beads mixed in. The braids swayed against her cheeks as she walked.

Reaching the table, she smiled. Her teeth shone in the sunlight. "We want to sign up."

"Are you guys lifeguards?" Lora asked.

"You bet," the taller boy said. He touched his nose. "This gave us away, huh? Kind of how a badge tells you someone's a policeman. "She," he gestured to the girl, "doesn't even need it. But we wear it so everyone will know we're lifeguards."

"And bow down when we pass," the girl added.

"Hi, I'm Tammy. Hi, I'm Lora," he read from their name tags. He laughed. "Hi, I'm Tom." From his sweatshirt pocket, he pulled a tube. "You guys want to be lifeguards,too?"

Giggling, they both nodded. With white paste from the tube, he coated their noses.

When he finished, he turned to his friends. "This is Evan," he gestured to the other boy, "and Mayday."

"Mayday?" Lora said.

"My real name's May," the girl said. "Mayday means the same thing as SOS. Like pilots call Mayday when their plane gets in trouble. When I started life-guarding, everyone began calling me that.''

Tom threw his arm around her. ''We know she'll always save us.''

Laughing, she twisted away, then punched his arm. ''You, I'd let drown.''

A car came into the parking lot. ''Looks like we better get on duty,'' Evan said. ''We don't usually all work at the same time,'' he told Tammy and Lora, ''but today's going to be really crowded.''

May picked up the pen and quickly signed the book. Evan followed. As Tom wrote his name, the other two started for the office.

''What does swim team involve?'' a woman asked.

Tammy looked up. A woman and two girls about seven or eight stood at the table.

''We start practices next Saturday,'' Lora said. ''Swim meets begin after school's out.''

''Do I have to be a good swimmer?'' one of the girls asked.

Lora shook her head no. ''The coach will help you. And it's lots of fun. We go to other swim clubs for some races. And we get special team suits. Purple, with a white lightning design.'' She ran her hand diagonally across her body.

The girl's eyes widened. ''Cool.'' She turned to her friend. ''Want to do it, Katie?''

Katie nodded.

''Please, Mom,'' the first girl said.

Her mother picked up the pen. ''I'll sign you both up.'' She looked at Katie. ''You check with your mom. She can call to cancel.''

"She won't," Katie said. "She thinks it's a good idea."

As the woman wrote in the book, Katie asked, "What's that white stuff on your noses?"

"Something to keep our noses from getting sunburned," Tammy said.

"It's what lifeguards wear," Lora added.

"Are you lifeguards?"

"Not yet," Lora said.

As those three left, others began lining up.

The next in line were two sixth-grade girls Tammy had seen at school. When they listed their age as twelve, Lora said, "With us and you two, we'll have enough for a relay team in our age group."

"What do we do for that?" the girl named Susan asked. She had wavy auburn hair and freckles.

"Like a relay race, only we swim instead of run," Lora said. "Are you guys very good swimmers?"

Susan waggled her hand. "So-so." She looked toward the dark-haired girl beside her. "How about you, Carmen?"

"I swim a lot, but I've never raced."

"What's your best stroke?"

"Crawl," Carmen said.

"In racing, they call that freestyle," Lora told her. "Well, really, in freestyle races you can do any stroke. Crawl is fastest, so that's what everyone does. That's why crawl ends up being called free."

"Then I guess my best stroke is free," Carmen said with a laugh.

"For one relay, everyone does freestyle," Lora said.

"The other relay has all four strokes: free, back, breast, and fly."

"I like to do backstroke," Susan said. She swung her arms as though swimming. "It's like I'm a floating windmill with my feet for an engine."

"I can swim breaststroke," Lora said. "Tammy swims fly."

"Butterfly?" Susan said. "That's a hard stroke."

Tammy shrugged and smiled. She hoped they couldn't tell what she was thinking—that she'd made a terrible mistake saying she liked fly.

As Carmen and Susan walked away, Lora nudged Tammy. "Don't look so worried. We'll practice every day till workouts start. You'll be good, I know."

Tammy forced another smile.

ten

In an hour, Tammy and Lora turned over the sign-up table to a boy about Melissa's age. His name was Jim Baxter. Bob Baxter's son, Tammy figured.

By then so many kids were in the water, Tammy thought she could walk across the pool using the bobbing heads as a bridge. Laughter and shouts filled the air. She saw Tom sitting in the elevated lifeguard chair near the diving board. Mayday guarded the little kids in the pool's shallow end. Evan sat in a beach chair near Tom.

Tammy and Lora headed for the locker room to get out of their clothes. They'd reached the door when Tammy heard her name called. She turned to see Melissa and Chuck entering the pool area. Melissa stood, scanning the area, then hurried to Tammy.

"My friend isn't here yet," she said. "Can I stick around you guys till someone comes?"

"Sure," Tammy said. "What about Chuck?"

"Why would I want to hang out with him?"

"Where's Mom?" Tammy asked.

"She got a call about that job at the junior college. They asked her to come in for another interview. This afternoon, because the head librarian is there today or something. I think she's going to get the job.''

Tammy and Melissa slapped hands. Melissa had complained about their mom's bad moods, too.

If she gets it, Tammy thought, *I can ask again for a kitten.*

Chuck joined them. He was wearing khaki shorts and a tan tank top. He carried a paperback book. ''How'd the sign-up go?''

''We got a lot of kids,'' Lora said. ''Most said they're not real good swimmers.''

Chuck shrugged. ''I understand you've got a good coach. He'll get you in shape.''

''Do you know him?'' Lora asked.

Chuck shook his head no. ''I do know he coaches at Firdale Swim and Tennis Club. It's a year-round team.''

''That's the one I'm joining in the fall,'' Lora said.

Chuck's eyebrows rose. ''You must be good. I understand the coaches there are pretty selective.''

''I've been swimming a long time,'' Lora told him. She looked at Tammy. ''This is good, having a coach from Firdale. If he sees you do well, then he'll let you join, too. We'd have so much fun.''

But I don't know if I want to join, Tammy thought. *And if they take only really good swimmers . . . even if I did want to, they wouldn't let me.* Tammy's chest tightened. She could lose her best friend. She took Lora's hand and squeezed gently. Lora squeezed back. Tammy couldn't let that happen.

From his pocket, Chuck pulled a bottle of suntan lotion and handed it to Tammy. ''Your mom said to put a lot of this on.'' He looked at her nose. ''Looks like you got started.''

''The lifeguards did it,'' Tammy said.

He tapped the bottle. ''Use this on the rest of you. I'm going to catch some rays. I'll see you later.'' Giving a small wave, he headed for one of the chaise longues.

The three girls entered the locker room and stripped down to their suits. Lora's was bright pink, with a multicolored design on the front. Carrying their towels, they headed back outside. Melissa stopped short at the doorway. She patted her hair, tugged at her suit.

''That lifeguard's cute,'' she said.

''His name's Tom,'' Tammy told her.

''How do you know?''

Tammy touched her nose. ''He's the one who did this.''

Melissa gave a big sigh.

''He's on swim team,'' Lora told Melissa.

''I'm still not joining.''

''Don't forget your swimming test,'' Tammy said.

Melissa frowned at her. ''I haven't forgotten it, Tammy. I'm just not going to think about it today.''

Dodging sunbathers, they reached the concrete bleachers. Melissa spread her towel on the deck. Taking the suntan lotion from Tammy, she spread it on her own legs and arms, then stretched out on her stomach. The sweet coconut smell wafted around them.

''Don't you want to practice swimming?'' Tammy asked.

''Stop nagging,'' Melissa said. ''Put some lotion on my back.''

When Tammy finished that, she and Lora rubbed on

lotion. As they did, Tammy studied the pool. A thick rope marked off two lap lanes for lap swimming. At the bottom of the pool, she saw black lines that also designated the lanes.

Lora jumped up. "Let's go."

"What do we do?" Tammy asked.

"Swim a couple laps to warm up. Then I'll watch how you swim. Maybe I can show you ways to go faster."

A couple laps? Tammy thought. *One is more than enough.*

Lora led Tammy to the pool's edge. This was the moment she'd both dreamed of and dreaded since she heard about swim team. As she stared down at the water, everything she'd learned about swimming drained from her head. She didn't want Lora to see she wasn't a good swimmer. "Maybe we should lie in the sun with Melissa for awhile."

"Come on, Tammy." Grabbing Tammy's hand, Lora jumped in.

Tammy had no choice but to go with her. Bubbles fizzed around Tammy as she went down, then bobbed up. Lora was there, holding on to the side and grinning at her.

Tammy wiped the water from her face. Head up, she swam to the edge. "Pretty sneaky," she said.

"I know, but you're in. Let's swim. I'll take the first lane."

Lora struck off. Tammy watched Lora's smooth free stroke for a moment, then followed. She used the black lines as a guide. Stroke, pull. Stroke, breathe, pull. Stroke, pull. She moved forward. As she took a breath, she saw the metal stairs on the pool side. That meant she'd swum half a lap. Her arms were getting tired, and she needed more air. Stroke, breathe, p-u-l-l-l, stroke, gulp air, p-u-l-l-l. Ahead, a black cross marked the end. She gave one last pull and reached it. She grabbed the side and held on. Her breaths came in gasps.

"You made it."

Tammy looked up. Lora sat on the edge. "Want to go again?" she asked.

Tammy took a deep breath. She looked over to the life guard chair. Tom glanced at her at the same moment. He gave her a thumbs up sign. "Not bad," he called.

He'd watched her. Her cheeks warmed. But he'd said she did okay. Her next breath was a sigh of pleasure.

"He's right," Lora said. "You need some conditioning, but you've got a pretty good stroke."

Laughing, Tammy looked the length of the pool. She'd conquered one whole lap. "Let's go," she said to Lora and started back.

This time her arms gave out before she reached the end. She flipped over and kicked herself to the finish. Lora stood on the deck, toweling her hair. Melissa wasn't there. Climbing out, Tammy glanced around. Her sister sat with another girl near the lifeguard chair.

"When I first started, my arms got tired, too," Lora said. She flexed an arm to show her muscle. "Pretty soon, your arms will look like mine."

Tammy held her arm up. Barely a bump of muscle. She wanted arms like Lora's. "How long does it take?" she asked.

"Depends on how much you practice."

"Let's swim another lap," Tammy said.

Just then, Susan and Carmen approached them. "Can we work out with you guys?" Carmen asked.

They swam laps off and on for the next hour. Then Carmen and Susan left to join some other friends.

At the concession stand, Mr. Baxter had begun cooking hot dogs. The aroma drifted around the pool. Tammy's stomach rumbled.

She and Lora bought hot dogs, chips, and a drink. They sat on the bleachers to eat. Chuck strolled over to them.

"I'm going home to check on your mom," he told Tammy. "She may already be back. I hope she gets the job."

The way he said it made Tammy think he was tired of her mom's bad mood, too.

"You're swimming looks real good, Tammy," he told her. "Who were the other two girls here?"

"The rest of our relay team," Tammy said.

"Tammy's going to swim fly for it," Lora added.

Tammy waited for him to say fly was hard. Instead, he said, "My favorite stroke. I bet you'll do well with it." He smiled at her.

This time she didn't try to hold her smile back. He was talking to her like he really cared how she felt. And it seemed more sincere because he wasn't saying these things in front of her mom.

He needed you to swim well, a small voice reminded her. *If you'd almost drowned, your mom would have been furious with him.*

"You girls look a little sunburned," he told them. "Get some more of that lotion on. You don't want to suffer tonight.'' He gazed over toward Melissa. ''I'd better check on her, too.''

''What does she have to do to stay off swim team?'' Tammy asked.

He thought a moment. ''Dive off the side, swim two laps of freestyle and one lap of backstroke, plus tread water five minutes.''

''That's a lot,'' Tammy said, thinking of how tired she'd gotten after one lap. ''You better tell her. She hasn't even practiced today.'' Tammy wanted Melissa to pass the test. If Chuck made her join swim team, she'd take her anger out on Tammy—all summer.

He nodded. ''I'll do that now.''

''He's nice,'' Lora said as she rubbed lotion on Tammy's back.

Tammy took her last bite of hot dog. ''I'm still hungry. I think I'll get another.''

eleven

Tammy and Melissa left the pool at about four o'clock.

"I got the job," their mom called as they walked into the house.

"No more gourmet meals," Melissa whispered.

Tammy grinned at the thought.

Their mom had been so bored at home, she'd begun cooking what she called "gourmet meals" for dinner. What Tammy called most of them was awful. Some of the names were interesting: *moussaka*, *bouillabaisse*, *sushi*. The dishes, however, contained weird things like eggplant and squid and seaweed.

Chuck praised the dinners, but Tammy had noticed he didn't always eat very much of them. She'd pushed her food around her plate. Most evenings, she joined Melissa in the kitchen later for peanut butter sandwiches. With their mom back to work, they could return to eating normal stuff: spaghetti, macaroni and cheese, hamburgers, tacos.

She and Melissa went to the back porch where their mom and Chuck sat. Smoke rose from their new charcoal barbecue.

"Hamburgers for dinner," their mom said. "Go shower and change so you'll be ready to eat."

Tammy yawned. Real food, finally, and she didn't feel like eating. She just wanted to go to bed.

Her mom took Tammy's hand. "Maybe you spent too many hours at the pool today."

"It's okay," Tammy said quickly. "I just need to get in better condition." She glanced at her sister. "Why don't you say that to Melissa, too? She looks really tired." After Chuck talked to her, Melissa had spent quite a bit of time in the water.

"I'm not tired," Melissa said. "I'm hungry, and I need a shower."

"I'm the same way," Tammy said. "I'm not tired, so don't say I am."

Her mother shook her head. "Both of you, go clean up."

As they left the room, Tammy heard her say, "Tammy always gets fussy when she's tired. I'm afraid this swimming thing may be too much for her."

Chuck's answer was spoken too quietly for Tammy to hear.

"I'm not fussy because I'm tired," she muttered to herself as she turned on the shower. "At least, not completely."

At the pool, she and Lora had tried working on fly in the shallow end, but it had been too crowded. Since they weren't swimming laps, Tom wouldn't let them swim in the lap lanes. Finally, they'd joined Melissa and her friend lying in the sun and listening to the radio.

Lora hadn't seemed to mind. Tammy did. She needed

a lot of practice on the stroke. Now, she had one less day to work on it.

She switched off the shower spray and climbed out. Dressing, she glanced at her blue bridesmaid's dress. *Act like a princess,* she told herself. Pasting a smile on her face, she went down to dinner.

Sunday, again the sun shone brightly, and again Tammy and Lora met to spend the day at the pool.

"I brought you something," Lora said when they went into the locker room. From inside her towel, she took two white swim caps. "I had an extra one. It'll keep your hair out of your face."

"Thanks," Tammy said, pulling on a cap. She looked in the mirror. Her face looked weird without hair around it. "That's what I'd look like if I were bald," she said.

Lora put on the other cap and joined her.

Tammy studied their reflections. "What if no one had hair? There wouldn't be ads on TV for shampoo, or barbershops or hair stylists. And you'd never have to comb out snarls. People could decorate their scalps anyway they wanted. Maybe there would be head fashions."

"And head stylists," Lora added, laughing.

"You could get appointments to have things painted on your head to match your clothes. Or paste jewels all over it when you went to a fancy party."

"How do you think of these weird ideas, Tammy?" Lora asked. "Like this and . . . the magic apple tree?"

Tammy shrugged. "Things just come in my head."

"With your imagination, maybe you should be a writer."

Tammy liked the thought. "That would be okay," Tammy said. "I like to make up stories."

The pool was still too crowded to work on butterfly. They swam laps instead; Lora, for speed; Tammy, to build up strength. Late in the afternoon, Lora's dad showed up with Ryan. While Ryan played in the shallow end, Mr. Davis timed Tammy and Lora with a stopwatch. He wrote their times on a piece of paper he stuck in his wallet.

"We'll check this at your first swim meet," he told Tammy.

Reading the times, she couldn't believe how much slower she was than Lora.

"Don't worry, Tammy," Lora said, then laughed. "I'm always saying 'Don't worry' to you, aren't I?"

"Some things are just important, Lora," Tammy told her.

Lora put an arm around Tammy's damp shoulder. "I know about swimming, Tammy. You have to trust me. When we start workouts, you'll take lots of seconds off your time."

"Lora's right, Tammy," Mr. Davis said. "You've got a good stroke. The stronger you get, the faster you'll go."

Tammy clenched her fist in front of her and looked at her arm. Had her muscle gotten a little bigger? "As fast as Lora?" she asked.

He laughed. "Maybe someday, you two will be swimming together in the Olympics."

The Olympics, Tammy thought. *Could that ever happen?*

Tammy held her clenched fist up. She patted the small

bulge in her arm. "I guess I have a lot to do before then."

Monday and Tuesday, after school, the girls went to the swim club. Those days, the pool was less crowded. For the hour and a half they were there, Lora helped Tammy with the butterfly stroke.

Everyone had been right, it was a hard stroke. Especially when she had to concentrate on doing everything perfectly. Like keeping her legs together when she did the kicks. Two kicks, one little, one big, to every sweep of her arms. She loved the feeling when her arms and legs worked together—the way she rose up out of the water with each stroke. She was almost like the leaping whales she'd seen at Sea World in San Diego.

Tuesday, Melissa joined them at the pool. While they practiced in the shallow end, she worked out in the lap lanes. Finally, at four-thirty, they went home. Melissa was excited because she'd swum the number of laps Chuck required of her. And Tammy felt good about the way her fly stroke was coming.

"Swimming sure makes me hungry," Melissa said as they reached their house.

Tammy agreed. Her stomach had been growling since they'd left the pool.

Chuck was in the kitchen when they arrived. "Your mom's working tonight," he told them. "My turn to cook dinner. I've planned a gourmet meal."

Melissa and Tammy exchanged glances.

"It'll be good," he assured them. "Something I used to have all the time in my bachelor days. Go ahead and get cleaned up. I'll call you when dinner's ready."

"I bet it'll be something with seaweed in it," Tammy said as she and Melissa went upstairs.

"Why can't he just get Chinese take-out?" Melissa grumbled. "I'm getting really tired of peanut butter sandwiches."

When Tammy got to her room, she heard a car motor. Out her window, she saw Chuck's car drive away. Probably went to get eels or chicken feet, she thought. Her mom had once mentioned seeing recipes for those items.

After the shower, Tammy dressed quickly. She was starving. Maybe she could sneak a sandwich before he returned.

She met Melissa at the top of the stairs. Melissa had had the same idea.

"Hurry," she said. "We can raid the refrigerator while he's gone."

Just then, Tammy heard the door from the garage open.

"Dinner," Chuck called.

Tammy and Melissa entered the kitchen cautiously. On the table sat plates, glasses, and two pizza boxes.

"Hey, great!" they said together and hurried to sit down.

Chuck pushed the larger box toward them. "Olives and pepperoni on Tammy's half. Extra cheese and pepperoni on Melissa's." He opened the smaller box. "The works for me."

"I thought you were cooking a gourmet meal," Melissa told him as she lifted out a piece of pizza.

From the counter, he took a plate of sliced carrots. "Here it is," he said, setting it in the middle of the table. "Gourmet all the way."

"Is this what you did in your bachelor days?" Tammy asked.

"You bet. The kitchen's a dangerous place. Hot pans to burn you. Boiling water to scald you. Sharp knives to slice off fingers." He held up his left hand. His pointer finger was bandaged. "Those carrots almost did me in."

Tammy giggled. Chuck's laughing with her gave her a warm feeling. It was like suddenly, she was okay. She didn't need to worry about swimming or keeping Lora's friendship. Those things would work out.

"So," Chuck continued, "how about we eat gourmet whenever I cook dinner?"

"Yes, yes," Tammy and Melissa both said.

He's really not so bad, Tammy thought as she took a bite of her pizza. *Maybe I should give him a chance.*

twelve

Later that evening, as Tammy climbed in bed, her mom opened the bedroom door. Light from the hallway shone in a triangle on the rug. She sat on Tammy's bed. "How'd your day go?" she asked.

Tammy scooted up to sit against the wooden headboard. Her mom stroked Tammy's hair. "In the dimness, your hair looks lighter. Must be the sun and chlorine."

"Lora's gets lighter, too. She said last year her hair turned almost white." Tammy squirmed against the hard back. She didn't want to talk about swimming with her mom. "How's your job?"

"So far, good," her mom said. "I like the people I work with."

Tammy sat silent for a moment. Her mom was in a good mood again. This was the time to ask for a kitten.

When she did, her mother said, "You're awfully busy with school and swimming. Do you have time to take care of one?"

"Oh, yes," Tammy said. "Besides, school's almost out. I'll have all day."

Her mother stood. "I'll talk to Chuck, see how he feels." She kissed Tammy good-night and left the room.

Smiling, Tammy snuggled under her covers. If her mom thought a kitten was a good idea, Chuck would agree, for sure.

Lora had a dentist appointment on Wednesday afternoon. Tammy went directly home after school. She let herself into the empty house. She liked it better when Melissa was there. She must have gone to a friend's. Or the pool. At least, in a few days, Tammy would have a kitten to greet her.

She fixed a quick snack of crackers and milk, then went into the spare bedroom. Several boxes left from moving were piled on the floor. Tammy took a small one to her room. Folding a hand towel, she lay it on the bottom of the box. Then she set the box on the floor by the head of her bed.

She pictured a kitten curled on the towel. She'd decided she wanted an orange cat. She and Lora had talked a lot about names. They'd finally chosen Marmalade.

She waited the rest of the week for her mom to bring up getting the kitten. Nothing was said. Tammy knew how busy her mom was with the new job and didn't want to nag her. She probably hadn't even had time to ask Chuck.

Saturday morning, the morning of the first practice, was cool and cloudy. Afraid her mom would stop her from going because of the weather, Tammy slipped out of the house before anyone else was up. Melissa didn't have to go. She'd passed Chuck's test the evening before.

Tammy met Lora at the pool. They sat on the bleachers with the rest of the team. In front of them stood the coach, Mr. Squire. He was about thirty-five, slender, with blond hair cut short. He wore a white sweatshirt, shorts, and sneakers. A whistle hung around his neck.

The week before, he'd phoned everyone who'd signed up for swim team. He'd divided them into groups based on their age and past experience. Tammy was to work out with the little kids; Lora, with the older ones. Except for the first day, the groups would swim at different times.

"No big deal, Tammy," Lora said when Tammy complained. "I'll swim with you, and you can swim in my group. Mr. Squire can't object to someone who's trying to swim better."

That morning, Mr. Squire took the older group to the lap end. While Evan lifeguarded, Tom and Mayday worked with the younger kids in the shallow part. They spent much of the hour swimming with kickboards. By the end of the session, Tammy's legs felt wobbly as cooked noodles.

When Tammy left the pool, Chuck's red pickup sat in the parking lot. He rolled down the window. "I thought you might be hungry," he said. "Want to get breakfast?"

"Sure," Tammy said. *Hungry* wasn't a big enough word for how her stomach felt.

He drove them to the local McDonald's. Chuck carried a white box in with him.

"What's that?" Tammy asked.

"I'll show you after we get our food."

He ordered scrambled eggs, a biscuit, and coffee. Tammy chose pancakes, sausage, and orange juice. They found an empty booth and sat down. She was so hungry, she started eating immediately. As she did, she glanced now and then at Chuck's box, sitting on the table. What could be in it?

She ate the final bite of pancake and set her fork down.

"Want another order?" he asked. "I know how hungry swimming can make you."

"Sure," Tammy said. "In a minute." She looked again at the box.

He drank some coffee. "I wanted to talk to you," he said. "You mom told me you'd like to get a kitten."

Tammy nodded slowly. The serious expression on his face suggested the news wasn't good. Her heart sank to her stomach. "It won't be any trouble," she said quickly. "I'll be responsible for it."

Chuck sighed. "I know you would be, Tammy. But I'm allergic to cats. If I'm around them, I have trouble breathing."

Now Tammy's heart dropped to her toes. "I'd keep it away from you. In my room. You'd never have to see it."

He shook his head. "I'm sorry. I just can't have one in the house."

Tammy fought back tears.

"I know how disappointed you are," he said, nudging the box toward her. "I got you something I hope will sort of make up for it."

Tammy lifted the lid. Inside sat a stuffed toy, a fluffy

white cat with blue eyes. It was just like the one Larry had given her when she was seven.

"Your mom said you once had one like it that you loved," Chuck said. "She said it got lost."

Tammy stared at the toy cat. The disappointment and sense of loss she'd felt when Larry left returned. How could she ever have thought she could trust Chuck? She set the lid on the box. "Thanks," she said. She stood. "I want to go home now."

"Tammy," he said, "what's wrong?"

"Nothing." She walked away, leaving the box on the table.

On the ride home, Tammy sat as close to the door as possible. She stared out the side window. At home, she found her mother in the backyard, watering. Tammy barely glanced at the sweet pea plants. They'd grown tall enough to reach the string trellis she and her mom had fashioned.

Her mom turned off the hose nozzle. "What's the matter, baby?" she asked.

"Chuck's allergic to cats." Tammy felt sure when her mom heard, she'd be furious at Chuck. Instead, her face grew sad.

"He told me. I'm so sorry."

On the way home, Tammy had thought about solutions to the problem. "We could build a room out here," she said. "Chuck could live in it."

Her mom gave a quick laugh. "I don't think that would be fair to Chuck."

"Then I'll live out here with the kitten."

Her mother put an arm around her. "Tammy, we're a family. No one's going to live outside."

Tammy twisted away. "Why'd you have to marry someone allergic to cats?"

"That's not one of the major deciding factors," her mom said.

"It would be for me," Tammy said. She stormed up the porch steps and into the house.

thirteen

Later that morning, as Tammy was getting ready to go to the pool, Melissa came into her room.

"I heard what happened," she said. "You sure have everyone upset."

"It's not my fault," Tammy told her. "Chuck's the allergic one."

"And you're the dumb one," Melissa said. "Chuck can't help being allergic. He feels really bad about this. Mom said he bought you a cute cat like the one you used to have. That was really sweet."

"Larry gave me the first one." Tammy pulled a sweatshirt on over her bathing suit.

"Chuck's not Larry, Tammy. Look how he supports you for swimming. And remember, he got you barbecued pork that day. He likes you a lot."

"If that were true, I'd have a kitten right now." Tammy put on her shorts.

Melissa's face was angry as she shook clenched fists. "You're tearing everyone apart, Tammy. Why don't you just grow up?"

Without a word, Tammy picked up her towel. She shoved past Melissa and out the bedroom door.

"Tammy, get back here!" Melissa cried, but Tammy hurried down the stairs and left the house.

The sun had burned off the morning clouds. Sunshine warmed her as she walked to the pool. She needed time to think. She was being childish. Melissa was right—Chuck couldn't help his allergy. Knowing that didn't make the hurt go away.

Maybe I could go live with Oma, Tammy thought. But she'd have to leave Lora. There'd be another new school to start. Staying here was better. She'd just stay away from Chuck.

Over the next weeks, Tammy settled into a routine at home. Evenings, after dinner, she went to her room, or if the weather was good, to the pool. She'd shoved the cat bed she'd made under her bed. Doing it, she whispered, "Good-bye, Marmalade." The tears had come then. She hadn't tried to stop them. She didn't know what happened to the white stuffed cat. When her mom tried to talk to her, Tammy told her she wasn't upset anymore.

Every weekday at five o'clock, she and Lora went to hour-long workouts at the pool. At that hour, the pool was closed to everyone but swim team members. Tammy swam with Lora and the older group Mondays, Wednesdays, and Fridays, plus Saturday mornings at seven o'clock.

The younger group worked out Tuesdays, Thursdays, and at eight o'clock Saturday mornings. At those practices, Lora spent that time helping Mr. Squire. He made the training fun. Some days, using the kickboards, the swimmers pretended they were racing motorboats. They putt-putted across the shallow end, about two-thirds of a lap. Winners got to choose something from the concession stand. Tammy, the oldest in the group, won the races every time. She refused the prizes.

"It's not fair for me to win," she said.

Once, Katie came in second after Tammy. Katie gave her half the candy bar.

"It's not right you never get anything," Katie said. "You work as hard as we do. And you're really good."

"Thanks," Tammy said, biting into the rich chocolate. Katie didn't know much about swimming, but the words were nice to hear anyway.

The older group practices included swimming a lot of laps as well as work on perfecting each stroke. In the beginning, Tammy always finished the laps last. The first time she noticed Mr. Squire watching her, she froze, afraid he'd tell her to get out of the pool. Instead, he smiled. "You're doing fine," he said. The words gave her more reason to work harder.

Both groups worked on diving off the starting blocks and on turns. On days they worked on starts, Lora asked Mr. Squire to leave two of the large white starting blocks in position when workout ended. She and Tammy continued to practice on them. Sometimes, Carmen and Susan joined them. Then they worked on relay starts, diving in just as the former swimmer touched the wall. Going too soon led to disqualification. Too late cost the team seconds.

Now, on her calendar, Tammy counted the days till school was out. Finally came the last day. Report cards were handed out, and Mr. Henderson said good-bye.

Tammy felt sorry to lose Mr. Henderson as a teacher. He'd made school fun and interesting. Before she and

Lora left the classroom, Tammy gave him a thank you note she'd written the night before. He read the note, then gave her a quick hug.

"Things like this are why I keep teaching," he said, tapping the note. "So what do you girls have planned for the summer?"

"We're on a swim team," Tammy said.

"Good for you." He smiled. "I swam for my high school team. If I'd started at your age, I would have been a lot better." He picked up a pile of textbooks from his desk. "Have a good summer," he said.

"And now," Lora said, once she and Tammy had left the school, "it's time to get down to serious swimming."

The following week, practices shifted to mornings at 7:00 for the older group, 8:00 for the younger. The first swim meet was scheduled for Thursday afternoon. The meet was a home meet, and they would swim against Sherwood Swim Club.

Each swimmer could compete in four events. Mr. Squire had signed Tammy up for the 200 Medley Relay and the 200 Free Relay. In both, each team member swam fifty yards, or two laps. Her other swims were the 100 Free and the 50 Fly.

"Your fly is coming along very well," Mr. Squire told her, "but I think the shortest race will be enough this time."

His praise swelled Tammy's chest. She'd worked so hard on the stroke. And swimming only two laps was fine. Lora had told her the judges disqualified swimmers who did the stroke wrong. Tammy knew when she got tired her legs didn't stay together enough.

She hoped her mom would have to work late on Thursday. If she came to the meet, she would see Tammy had to swim four laps in the 100 Free. Lora would swim even more distance. The 200 Free, eight laps.

To Tammy's dismay, her mom had that night off. "I'll finally get to see your swimming," she said. "Chuck's told me how well you're doing."

Chuck swam after work every day. Sometimes, during the weeks that the practices were at five, he'd gotten to the pool before swim practice finished. Tammy had noticed him watching from the bleachers.

Thursday morning, no workout was planned. Lying in bed Wednesday night, she imagined everything that could go wrong at the meet. She'd start before the starter gun went off. She'd fall off the starting block. She'd miss touching the end when she turned. She'd do the wrong stroke. None of those worries prepared her for what did happen. In the middle of the night, she woke with an earache.

fourteen

The earache started as a small pain at first. As the night progressed, the hurting grew worse. Her tension only added to it. She remembered the last earache she had. It had meant a trip to the doctor, medicine, and staying in bed for two days. If her mom knew about this one, she'd never allow Tammy to swim.

But I have to, she thought. *I can't let the relay team down. And besides, this is my very first swim meet. I've waited two months for it.*

Climbing out of bed, she tiptoed through the dark house to the bathroom. She took some pain medicine. It dulled the ache so she could go back to sleep.

The hurting got her out of bed early. She put on her robe and slippers and went to the kitchen. Her mom sat there, eating a bowl of cereal. The morning was overcast; she'd turned the kitchen light on to brighten the room.

"How are you this morning?" she asked Tammy.

"Just fine, just fine," Tammy said quickly. She put a piece of bread in the toaster and pushed the lever down.

"I hope the clouds burn off by this afternoon for your meet."

"Me, too," Tammy said.

Her mom studied her. "You sound a little uptight. Is something bothering you?"

Tammy's shoulders tensed. She shook her head hard. Doing that made her ear hurt more. To hide her wince, she turned quickly back to the toaster. The scent of toasted bread rose from it.

"A little worried about the meet?" her mom asked.

Good, Tammy thought. *She's given me an excuse.* "Yeah, I guess I am."

Standing, her mom put her hands on Tammy's shoulders and gave a small squeeze. "You'll do just fine, I know."

"Thanks, Mom." The toast popped up. Tammy concentrated on spreading butter on it.

Her mother set her dishes in the dishwasher. She left the room to finish getting ready for work. Tammy breathed a sigh of relief.

Lora came over midmorning. Tammy was alone in the house. Melissa had spent the previous night with a friend and hadn't come home yet. Tammy led Lora outside to check on the sweet peas. Buds, some just starting to open, covered the plants.

"What's the matter, Tammy?" Lora asked. Her face was concerned.

"What do you mean?"

Lora shrugged. "You seem really tense. Not your usual worried kind of tense. Like something's really bothering you."

Tammy crouched before the sweet peas. Tendrils curled tightly around the trellis. The plants had grown almost to the top string. She put a hand to her right ear. "My ear hurts so bad I want to scream."

Lora grimaced. "Swimmer's ear, I bet. I've had that. It's awful."

"Swimmer's ear?" Tammy repeated.

"It happens because you get water in your ears from swimming. Then bacteria grow in them and make them hurt. My mom mixes up something with vinegar and drops that in my ears when I get it. She's already had to do it for Ryan. Tell your mom. She'll call the doctor."

"I can't. If she knew, she wouldn't let me swim."

Lora's eyes widened. "We can't let that happen. My mom will fix it." She took Tammy's arm. "Let's go to my house."

Once there, she explained the problem to her mom.

"No cough, no cold?" she asked. They stood in the kitchen. She was bathing Emily in a small blue bathtub.

Tammy shook her head no.

"Lora's right. It sounds like swimmer's ear. I've still got some stuff mixed up for it." She rubbed some shampoo on Emily's fuzz of blonde hair. The baby babbled and kicked her feet.

"It's in the medicine cabinet," Mrs. Davis told Lora. "You know the bottle. Bring the dropper, too." She scooped water over Emily's head. Emily squealed with pleasure.

Removing her from the bath, Mrs. Davis wrapped her in a soft, white terry-cloth towel. One of its corners was shaped to be a hood. It covered Emily's head and drooped down on her forehead almost to her eyes. Looking at her, Tammy laughed. That made her ear hurt more. Quickly, she pressed a hand against it.

Tammy followed Mrs. Davis into Emily's room. Lora met them there. While she sat in the rocker with Emily, Mrs. Davis pressed around Tammy's neck. "No swollen glands," she said.

She tilted Tammy's head and put some of the solution in one ear, then the other. The cold drops tickled. The sharp vinegary odor reminded Tammy of salad dressing. "Now I know how lettuce feels," she said.

"You probably shouldn't swim today," Mrs. Davis told her.

"Mom," Lora said.

Her mother laughed. "That's like telling the sun not to come up, I know. But you need to keep your inner ears dry, Tammy. Get some earplugs. I know they sell them at the pool."

"Yeah, Tammy," Lora agreed. "I've done that. It'll work."

And Mom won't ever know, Tammy thought. "Okay," she said.

Mrs. Davis poured some of the solution in a small bottle. She gave that and the dropper to Tammy, along with instructions on how to use it.

Now that Tammy's concern about her ear had been dealt with, she felt free to worry about the meet. "Maybe we should go to the pool and practice," she told Lora.

"Tammy, you don't want to get all worn out before the races," Lora said.

Ryan, still in pajamas, came into the room. Tammy had seen him earlier in the family room watching TV.

"When do we swim?" he asked.

"Not till four o'clock," Lora told him.

''Do I have to go?'' he asked.

Tammy crouched before him. Tiny red, blue, and yellow dinosaurs marched across the fabric of his pajamas.

''Are you worried about the race?'' she asked.

He gazed down at his bare feet. ''Maybe.''

''Me, too,'' she told him.

''Do you think you won't get to the end?'' he asked.

''I used to worry about that. But I found out if I just kept moving my arms, I'd reach it.''

He frowned. ''It's a l-o-o-o-ng way.''

''I know. But we're tough.''

He flexed his arm muscles. ''Yeah, we are.'' Turning to his mother he asked, ''How much longer to wait?''

''Mom,'' Lora said. ''This is getting too tense. Could we go to a movie to kill time?''

Her mom looked up from the changing table where she was dressing Emily. ''If you find something good, I'll take you.''

Lora and Tammy got out the morning newspaper. They found a movie they'd all like. It ended at 2:30. They had to be at the pool at 3:00 for warm-up.

Watching the movie kept Tammy's mind off her ear and the swim meet. When it was over, Mrs. Davis stopped at Tammy's house so she could get her team suit. The purple suits had been handed out at practice the day before.

They dressed at Lora's. Tammy loved the suit, the way the white lightning flash dashed across the front.

''Now we're really twins,'' Lora said as they checked their reflections in the mirror. Lora raised her arm and made a fist. Tammy did the same. ''Look, Tammy,'' Lora said. ''We even have muscles that match.''

Lora was right, Tammy realized. Grinning, she flexed her arm several times, watching the muscle move up and down.

Lora's mom drove them to the pool. Except to swim team members, it was closed for swimming during the meet. Tammy stopped by the office and bought earplugs. Then they headed for the bleachers where the rest of the team sat. Everyone wore the purple team suit.

As they approached, Tammy slowed. She made a fist, held it to her mouth and spoke into it. "Crestview tour members, today you're in luck. We are coming up on a herd of purple-suited swimmers. Be very quiet as we move forward. We don't want to frighten them. They're very shy animals, found most often hanging around a watering hole. As we see them now."

Lora giggled. "You're silly, Tammy."

They climbed up to the top row of bleachers and sat on their towels. Below them, Mr. Squire paced before the group. The sun had finally come out. The calm pool water gleamed in the light. Cords holding small triangular flags had been stretched high across the lap lanes a few yards from each end. Backstrokers used them to judge the distance left to go before they made their turns. No breeze moved the multi-colored flags.

"Before we start warm-up," he said, "I want to talk about the meet. Today is the day you'll be setting your times. The time you get in each race determines which lane you'll swim in next meet. It also gives you something to go after. Next time, you'd like to swim a little faster. In that respect, in each meet, you're swimming against yourself."

He bent to Katie, seated on the lowest bleacher. "Do you understand what I'm saying?"

She frowned, then nodded. "Every week I want to beat myself."

He laughed. "That's a very good way to put it." He patted her head, then addressed the group again.

"You're also swimming against the other team for points. You get points every time you place in the top six. Ribbons, also, for the top three. The team with the most points at the end of the meet wins. Now I know we're a brand-new team, but we've got some very good swimmers. Mayday, Tom, Evan, Lora, to name a few. A lot more are coming on strong. We have as good a chance as the other teams of winning. More important than winning, though, is improving every week. If you do that, winning will get easier." He paused. "Most important is having fun."

Tammy glanced around at the other swimmers. They sat as quietly as she. Were the feelings of excitement, worry, *scaredness* fizzing inside them, too? She wanted to jump in the water and get started. She wanted to jump up and run home. She began tapping her fingers on her thigh.

Lora put a hand on Tammy's. "Stop worrying," she whispered.

Mr. Squire gestured to six trophies standing near the diving board. "Bring those here, would you, Tom? And Evan?"

The boys carried them to him, setting them at his feet. Each was gold, about two feet tall, with a gold statue of a swimmer on top. Three were girls; three, boys.

"These are our team trophies," he said. "At the end of the season, I'll choose the two best swimmers, two most improved swimmers, and two most inspirational swimmers. A boy and a girl for each category. We'll engrave the names on the trophies. They'll be kept in the office for everyone to see. Those chosen will also get a small trophy to take home."

Tammy stared at the gleaming golden trophies. The big kids would probably win for best swimmers. Tom, maybe, and Mayday. She was really good. Lora had a chance for most inspirational girl. She worked a lot with the kids in the younger group. The most improved girl would be the only one Tammy had a chance at. But Susan, for one, had gotten a lot better since they started. So had some of the little kids. She pictured *Tammy Tallman* engraved in the gold. *I'll try for it anyway,* she thought. *From now on, I'll work even harder. And if Mr. Squire sees me doing that, he might let me join Firdale Swim Team.*

fifteen

Mr. Squire lined everyone up for warm-up. The little kids went to the shallow part; the older ones to the lap lanes. They swam in groups of six, each set diving off the starting blocks when the one before reached the lap end.

Tammy swam with her earplugs. It seemed strange, not hearing the fizzy bubbling sounds of the water. By the time warm-up finished, the other team had arrived. It had at least twice as many members as Crestview did. Sherwood Swim Club members wore red suits. The girls' suits had three white stripes at the waist.

"The Red-Suited Swimmers meet the Purple-Suited Swimmers," Lora said as she patted herself dry. "Sounds like a science fiction movie. Like a battle for the planet, or something."

Tammy raised her fist. "First the watering hole, then the world."

Giggling, they went into the locker room. Tammy took the dropper and bottle of ear solution from her locker. Standing before the mirror, she tipped her head to put the drops in her ear.

The first drop felt cold and made her shiver. As she

squeezed out the second drop, she heard her mother's voice.

"Tammy, what are you doing?"

Tammy froze.

Her mom's reflection appeared in the mirror. Her expression showed her upset. She took the dropper out of Tammy's hand. Standing behind her, Lora rolled her eyes.

Tammy's mom sniffed the solution. "What's this? It smells like vinegar."

"It's for swimmer's ear," Tammy said in a small voice.

Her mom's eyebrows rose. "What?"

Tammy explained about her earache and Lora's mom.

"You can't swim when you have an earache," Tammy's mother said. "We have to get a doctor to check you. Come on, we'll go right now."

"I can't miss the meet, Mom."

"Tammy, now."

Tammy knew that tone of voice. Her shoulders drooped. What would Mr. Squire think if she left the meet? Her relay team? Her eyes met Lora's in the mirror. "I'm sorry."

Lora took Tammy's hand. "It's okay."

But it's not. The words screamed inside Tammy's head.

With Lora, she followed her mom outside. Chuck stood there. He looked from Tammy to her mom. "What's the matter?"

Tammy's mom held out the bottle of solution. "An earache. She's trying to cure it with vinegar."

Chuck gazed at Tammy. "Swimmer's ear?"

"That's what Lora's mom said." She wondered how Chuck knew about swimmer's ear.

"I wouldn't worry about it," he said to her mom. "We'll get earplugs to keep her ears dry."

"I got some," Tammy said. "Mrs. Davis said to."

"You need a doctor," her mother insisted.

"My mom *is* a doctor," Lora said. "She's taking a break because of Emily."

Chuck took the solution and dropper from Tammy's mother and handed them to Tammy. He put an arm around her mom's waist. "Come on, let's go get seats to watch the meet."

They walked away. Tammy knew by her mom's set shoulders how bothered she was. She plopped into a deck chair. "Whew," she said, "that was close."

"Good thing you have Chuck," Lora said.

"Yeah," Tammy said. She didn't know what else to say.

Over the loudspeaker, Mr. Squire announced the meet was starting. The 200 Freestyle, Lora's race, came first. Because of its length, the youngest age group for this race was eleven-twelve. That meant Lora swam in the first heat.

Tammy went with her to the scorer's table to pick up her time card. They checked the heat sheet. It listed each race, the swimmers, their times and lanes. Lora swam in lane three, the lane for the swimmer with the fastest entering time. The slowest swam in lane six. Each lane had a parent timing. Other parents watched to see that the swimmers did the strokes and turns correctly. If they didn't, they were disqualified.

Final call for the heat sounded. Lora pulled on her

swim cap. "Wish me luck," she said. Watching her step up on the starting block, Tammy felt excitement welling up inside. She wanted to be up there. She didn't want to wait for her turn. She was ready right then.

The six swimmers took their positions. The starting box beeped. All six dove.

Susan and Carmen joined Tammy. They yelled for Lora. She reached the end first, flipped and started back. By the fifth lap, she was a lap ahead of two of the other swimmers.

Completing the eighth lap well in front, she touched and pulled herself from the pool. Water streamed from her as she checked with the timer. Hearing her time, she broke into a broad grin.

Tammy followed her to where her mom and dad sat. Ryan was with them. Emily sat on Mrs. Davis's lap.

"I got my best time ever," Lora told them. "I might have good enough time to swim in the next age group."

"What's that mean?" Tammy asked.

"To swim with thirteen-fourteen year olds, you have to get a certain time. If I have that, next meet, I can race in that race."

"If I get a really bad time, can I swim with the ten year olds?"

Lora laughed. "Doesn't work that way."

Lora's dad pulled the piece of paper from his wallet. "Remember this, Tammy? Your times when you started?"

Tammy nodded.

"I think you'll be surprised at the difference between then and now."

"I hope so," Tammy said.

"How's your ear?" Mrs. Davis asked her.

The pain had settled into a dull ache Tammy had ignored. "Not as bad," she said.

They stayed and watched the rest of the 200 Freestyle heats. They cheered for Mayday when she swam, and for Tom and Evan. Mayday took first, well ahead of the others. Tom did the same. Evan came in third.

The next race was the 100 Medley Relay. They met Susan and Carmen at the scorers' table. As they waited for the younger kids to swim, Carmen kept up a constant chatter concerning her worry about the race. Her words churned in Tammy's stomach.

Finally came their heat. Sherwood Swim Club was big enough to have three eleven-twelve relay teams. Tammy's team swam in lane five. Backstrokers went first in the medley relay. Susan took her position in the water, feet and hands against the pool end.

The starter went off, and the swimmers' arms thrust up and back.

"Go, Susan!" they yelled as she moved away from them.

Susan was third to reach the end. She turned and started back. Breaststroke came next. Lora took her position on the block. When Susan touched, Lora dove in. Her head bobbed up with each breaststroke. She'd passed the second-place swimmer before she turned. She came out of the turn half a lap ahead.

Heart thumping with excitement, Tammy climbed on the block. Preparing to dive, she kept her eyes riveted on Lora's hands. They thrust forward, then swept back. Closer. Closer. So hard to wait. Forward, back. Forward, back. Forward. Touch!

"Go for it, Tammy!" Chuck's shout followed her into the water.

sixteen

Bubbles whirled around Tammy as she surfaced. Over and over, she reminded herself to keep her legs together. She didn't want to be disqualified. When she reached the end, she remembered to touch with both hands as she turned. In the next lane, another swimmer came toward her. She wasn't last then. She swam faster.

Nearing the starting point, she stroked harder. A final strong kick propelled her to the end. She grabbed the pool ledge and hung on. Behind her, Carmen had splashed in. Tammy wiped the water from her face and pulled herself out.

Lora hugged her. "You kept us in second place."

Tammy glanced to her side. The third-place swimmer was out of the water, too. "I lost some of the time you caught up," she told Lora.

"Not that much," Lora said.

Carmen lost time in the first lap. The lane four swimmer was catching her.

"Go, Carmen, go," Tammy screamed.

Carmen touched a split second before the other swimmer.

"Sorry, guys," she said when she found out.

"Hey, don't worry," Lora told her. "We took third." They'd left the starting blocks and stood near the bleachers. "We'll be even stronger next week."

Mr. Squire came over to them. "You girls did very well." He looked toward Tammy. "Your last push guaranteed third place."

Tammy couldn't stop the smile the compliment brought.

"Sherwood's been building their team for several years," Mr. Squire continued. "Most of those swimmers have at least triple-A time. To come in third against them is quite an accomplishment. I'll have white ribbons for you tomorrow."

Lora laughed. "Next week, we're going for second." The four slapped hands.

"What's triple-A time?" Tammy asked when he'd left.

"A time you need to qualify for certain meets," Lora explained. "You need a better time to go to state, even better for regionals and nationals. Finally, there's the Olympics."

"Do you have triple A?" Tammy asked.

"Yeah. I almost have regional time. That means I get to go to out-of-state meets. They're really fun."

I want to do that, too, Tammy thought.

Tammy's mom called her. Her mom and Chuck sat in the second row of bleachers. She beckoned to Tammy.

She picked up her towel from the chair she'd laid it on. Sun had heated the fabric. She wrapped it around her, enjoying its warmth, and joined them.

"We took third," she said.

"Your race was the key, you know," Chuck said.

He smiled at her, and she smiled back. She didn't have to trust him to appreciate the praise.

Her mother put an arm around Tammy's shoulders. "That stroke you did looks like a lot of work," she said. "Are you tired?"

Tammy shook her head no. "We've been practicing. I'm getting stronger."

"How about your ear?"

"It's okay," Tammy said. "I think the drops are working."

The scent of barbecued hamburgers rose to her. She looked down to see Mr. Baxter cooking before the concession stand. He wore a tall white chef's hat and a white apron. On the front, in red letters, were the words I LIVE TO BARBECUE.

"You hungry?" her mom asked.

"A little," Tammy said. "And thirsty."

Her mother picked up her pocketbook.

"I can't eat," Tammy said. "I have more races."

"More? I'd say that was enough."

Tammy swallowed hard. She'd known her mom would react this way. "Mom, I race four times. I do another butterfly, a 100 free, and the free relay."

"How far is 100?"

"Four laps," Tammy said.

"That's too much," her mom said. "You're just a little girl."

Tammy gave a big sigh. "Lora just swam eight laps."

"She's been training for this," Chuck said. "If the coach didn't think she could do it, he wouldn't let her."

Just then, Lora called Tammy's name. Relieved, Tammy stood. From the purse, her mother pulled some change. She gave it to Tammy. "Get something to drink," she said.

"Thanks, Mom." Tammy kissed her mom's cheek, then climbed down to Lora.

The medley relays were still going on. After them came the I.M.s, the individual medley in which each swimmer swam all four strokes.

The girls bought some juice, then found a quiet place and laid out their towels. Lora had brought a deck of cards, and they started a game of hearts. Susan and Carmen joined them. They sat in the late afternoon sun until 50 backstroke was called. The 50 breaststroke followed that. Ryan and Lora would swim in different heats of that race. For his age, the distance was reduced to one lap, twenty-five yards.

Tammy and Lora met Lora's dad at lane end. At the other, Ryan climbed on a starting block. He was the smallest of the swimmers. His expression showed his total concentration. The swimmers dived with the beep.

Ryan moved forward slowly, his head rising with each stroke. He reached halfway and stopped, treading water. Evan, who was working as lifeguard then, moved to the side of the pool.

"Come on, Ryan," Mr. Davis yelled, "you can do it."

Tammy watched, her heart in her throat. Ryan was out there because she'd told him he could make it. What if he sank? What if he drowned? "Keep moving your arms," she shouted. "Don't give up. You'll get here."

His arms thrust forward, pulled back to move him

ahead. To Tammy, it felt like watching a snail move. Beside her, Lora called, "Pull . . . pull . . . pull."

Ryan reached the end. Everyone in the bleachers clapped as his dad pulled him from the water. Lora wrapped a towel around him.

He looked up at Tammy. "You were right," he said, then turned to his dad. "I don't want to swim anymore. I want to play soccer."

Laughing, Mr. Davis picked him up. "Let's go talk about it."

Lora's heat came soon after. Again, she touched well ahead of her competitors.

Then it was Tammy's turn for the 100 Free. When her heat was called, she handed the timer her scorecard. At the beep, she went into the water. Her stroke felt smooth, but her turns, clumsy. Neither time did she get the push off she needed. Finishing the heat, she saw Lora's dad standing by the block. He held out the paper from his wallet. She left the pool and checked her time. She'd cut ten seconds from the time on the paper. *If my turns had gone better,* she thought, *I would have been faster.* Next week, she'd practice turns more.

"Three more seconds and you'll have triple A-time," Lora said.

"How'd I do in this race?" Tammy asked.

"Looks like third," Mr. Davis told her.

The 50 Fly followed right after. That race didn't go as well for Tammy. When she finished, she learned she'd been disqualified because she hadn't kept her legs together for the entire race. Looking at the D.Q. for "disqualified" written on the timecard, Tammy vowed she wouldn't let that happen again.

They played cards until the Free Relay was called. Carmen swam first. She touched fourth. Tammy followed. Her ear hurt; her arms were tired. She couldn't let the team down—Susan, who swam after her, wasn't that great at free. Tammy had to move them up. She pulled and kicked as hard as she could. Susan jumped in as Tammy touched.

Her arms lacked the strength to boost her from the pool. Lora reached down and helped her out. Tammy stood, trying to dry herself with her damp towel.

"We're in third place," Lora said. "You did great."

Susan's swim put them back to fourth, but Lora wasted no time in catching them up.

"Another good race," Mr. Squire told them.

Third place three times, Tammy thought. She'd have three white ribbons to put on her bulletin board.

Chuck and her mom joined them. Tammy searched her mother's face. Would she say Tammy had to quit?

Her mom tugged the towel tighter around Tammy. "Looks like you should bring two towels next week."

Tammy released a relieved sigh. "Guess so," she agreed.

Lora's parents came up to them. Mrs. Davis carried Emily. She was sound asleep. Ryan held his dad's hand. "The team's going out for pizza," Mr. Davis said.

"I'm kind of tired," Tammy said. She didn't mention her aching ear. "I want to go home and call Oma."

Over the past weeks, she'd kept her grandmother informed about her swimming. Tammy had promised to call after the meet.

When Tammy did call, she told Oma about the three ribbons.

"*Ach, Liebchen,*" Oma said, "how proud I am. I wish I could have been there."

"Me, too," Tammy said. "Can you come visit us?"

"In the winter," Oma said. "When I get back from Germany."

Oma was taking a four-month trip to Germany in the fall.

"Then you can show me how you swim," Oma told her.

If I'm on Firdale Swim Team. Tammy clenched her fists. *I will be. I have to be.*

seventeen

The next six weeks passed quickly. Tammy's earache cleared up. The sweet peas flowered. Tammy spotted bouquets around the house. The apples grew bigger every day. Chuck said they were Jonathans. He rubbed his stomach. "Great for pies and applesauce."

Some warm nights, Tammy and Lora slept outside in Tammy's backyard. Melissa and her friend Elena sometimes joined them. Tammy loved the feel of the soft night air. Around her, like dashes of light, pale moths flitted through the dusk. When the night grew dark, the girls climbed in their sleeping bags. They searched for constellations in the star-filled sky. Tammy learned to find the Big Dipper. And Cygna, the Swan, with its star-wings.

She told them ghost stories. She made them as creepy as she could. She loved it when Lora said a story made her scalp prickle or gave her shivers. The best time came one night when Melissa got so scared she went inside to sleep.

Swim practice continued every weekday morning. Sometimes, after workout, they stopped at the office. The swim team trophies stood on one of the shelves.

"Sure would look nice with your names on it," Ms. Carter always told them.

Tammy wondered if she said that to everyone who stopped to look at the trophies.

Once, on the way home, Lora said, "Ms. Carter's right. Our names would look good on those."

They paused to watch roofers work on one of the unfinished houses. The scent of cedar hung in the warm air.

"I think I have a chance for Most Inspirational," Lora said.

"For sure," Tammy said. "Mr. Squire's always talking about how much you help everyone."

"And you can probably get Most Improved."

An image of the trophy rose in Tammy's head. To win it would be so fantastic. "Do you really think so?" They'd started walking again.

"Look at how much better you are. I bet if you got that, Mr. Squire would ask you to join Firdale for sure."

"Then I guess I better go for it." Arms out, Tammy twirled forward down the walk. Lora whirled after her.

Swim meets occurred every Thursday afternoon. Half of them were away meets, and the team traveled to other pools. During one meet, a summer storm darkened the day. The coaches stopped the races and got everyone out of the pool. They stood under cover, while overhead, lightning flashed and thunder boomed. The pool water danced in the downpour. If a pool's hit by lightning, Tammy learned, anyone in it will be electrocuted. The thought of that happening made her shivery. Waiting, she stayed far from the water.

As Lora had predicted, the girls began to place second

in the medley relay. Tammy's times improved, too. Red ribbons joined the white ones on her bulletin board. Each time she pinned one up, she vowed that soon she'd be adding blue ones.

One day after practice, Mr. Squire said, "Tammy, with the right training, you could become a very good fly swimmer."

"I like that idea," she said. She hoped he'd say she could get the help at Firdale Swim and Tennis Club.

Instead, he simply nodded and left to talk to Mayday.

Though Tammy's mother didn't make all the meets, Chuck didn't miss any. Tammy hadn't realized she depended on his being there until he came late one day. When that happened, she'd felt the way she had when Larry left. Chuck showed up half an hour later, all apologies. Her relief surprised her. Was Melissa right? Could Tammy trust him?

Tammy had seen Mr. Squire talking to Chuck at some of the meets. One day after the races, Chuck told her the coach thought she had potential as a swimmer.

"What's that mean?" Tammy asked.

"He thinks you have the ability to be very good. And he's impressed with how hard you work. Have you ever thought of swimming year-round, like Lora?"

"Yeah, but I don't know if Mom would let me."

Chuck hadn't said anymore. He'd just looked thoughtful.

The final meet of the summer was held at Crestview. This would be Tammy's last chance to earn a blue ribbon. And to get triple-A time in free. She'd been close to triple-A time the last meet, missing it by only half a second.

Mr. Squire had talked to her briefly after that meet. "I have a feeling about you next week," he'd told her. "Triple-A time in free is within your grasp."

She'd held up her hand, then closed it as though she were catching something. "Got it," she said.

He laughed. "If it happens, it could open a door for you."

She'd stared at him, confused. He'd just patted her shoulder and turned away.

Later, Tammy told Lora what he'd said. "What does he mean, open a door?" Tammy asked.

Lora grabbed Tammy's hands. "I bet he means a door to Firdale Swim Team." She shook Tammy's arms up and down. "I'm so excited. We'll get to be together."

If I get triple-A time, Tammy had thought. *If my mom lets me join*. Two big, big ifs.

The team they'd swum against that day was the best team in the league. She'd had no chance of taking first in any of the heats. The opposing team in the final meet was not as strong.

Before leaving for the race, Tammy touched her bridesmaid's dress. "I'll swim like a princess," she promised. Leaving her room, she went to the back yard. There, she rubbed the smooth trunk of the apple tree. "Magic tree," she whispered, "make me the best swimmer today."

She met Lora at the pool. Again, their relay team took second in the medley relay. Carmen still couldn't hold the lead.

After the relay, Tammy tried to settle down and wait for the 100 Free. She and Lora sat with Lora's mom for awhile. They carried Emily around the pool. She burbled and laughed, and everyone wanted to see her. When Emily started fussing, they returned her to her mother. Then, Tammy paced the pool area until her 100 Free heat was called.

Tammy climbed on the block. She took position. The beep sounded. *Princess Tammy*, she thought as she dove in.

She did her first turn too early. She didn't get a good push off the wall. *I've lost it,* she thought as she surfaced. Her distress made her stroke uneven, the rhythm ragged. *Don't panic,* she told herself. *Focus. Pull. Pull. Keep your kick strong. Turn coming. Don't rush it. Now!*

The turn was perfect. She surged forward, made another good turn and took off, sprinting for the finish.

As she climbed out, Lora reached around the timer and took Tammy's card. Tammy grabbed it away. She read it once, then again to make sure.

"Yes!" she screamed. "Yes, yes, yes." She and the magic tree and the princess dress had triple-A time.

She squeezed out between the timers. Laughing, Lora grabbed her and spun her round and round. Mr. Squire approached them. A wide smile creased his face.

"Triple-A time," Tammy told him.

"I guessed that," he said, laughing. "You also won the race."

Tammy took a deep breath. Her first blue ribbon.

At five o'clock the following day, swim team members, their families, Ms. Carter and Mr. Squire gathered at the grassy open area behind the office and locker rooms. They'd come for the Crestview Swim Team Awards Banquet.

Several barbecues had been set up. Chuck, along with Mr. Baxter and some other parents would cook hamburgers and hot dogs for everyone. Already, the air was hazy with the smoke.

Tammy, Melissa and their mom covered one of the picnic tables with a blue vinyl tablecloth. Lora's mom spread out a blanket on the ground for Emily. Ryan sat beside her, shaking a rattle.

Lora, Melissa and Tammy set out the food they'd brought—potato salad, pickles, chips, carrot sticks, cans of pop, as well as ketchup and mustard. Tammy and Lora had made a chocolate sheet cake that afternoon. They'd decorated it with sugar sprinkle goldfish and the letters T and L in blue. They added the cake to the other food.

"When will Mr. Squire announce the awards?" Tammy asked Lora as they stood in line at the barbecue. The scent of cooking meat wafted around them.

Mr. Baxter set a hamburger on Lora's plate. "Probably after dinner," she answered. "They always make you wait."

After the meet, the evening before, Tammy had stopped at the office to look at the trophies. They'd been gone.

"They're at the engravers for the names," Ms. Carter said. "Maybe yours."

"Do you know who?" Tammy asked.

Ms. Carter grinned. "Why spoil the surprise?"

"I don't like surprises," Tammy said.

Laughing, Ms. Carter turned back to the papers she was working on.

Tammy had just finished her second hot dog when Mr. Squire asked for everyone's attention. He stood in the middle of the area, by one of the picnic tables. On it, black plastic hid the six trophies.

eighteen

Tammy scooted over as Chuck came to the table. He set down a plate with two hamburgers. Catching Tammy's eye, he smiled at her. She felt too nervous to smile back.

"I'd like to welcome you all to our first annual swim team banquet," Mr. Squire said. "As most of you know, our team came in sixth in a league of six teams. That doesn't mean we did all that badly. We just didn't have enough swimmers to get the extra points we needed. Next year, when the rest of the homes are finished, we'll have a team twice as big. And the way these kids worked this year, if they all come back, we have a good chance of moving up."

Mr. Squire placed a hand on the trophies beside him. "I know everyone is curious about whose names are on these. I want all of you to understand how difficult the decisions were. The names on here represent the hard work of everyone on our team."

Why doesn't he stop talking? Tammy thought. She sat, shoulders tense, eyes straight ahead. In her lap, fingers on both hands were crossed. Lora's elbow nudged her. Lora was tying a knot in her own hair. Tammy took Lora's other hand and squeezed.

"Stop worrying," Tammy said.

"That's what I'm supposed to say," Lora whispered.

"The first trophies are for the most inspirational," Mr. Squire went on. "I looked for the kids who spent time helping other swimmers to achieve their best." He reached into the plastic and pulled out a trophy. "The girl whose name is on this was often my assistant coach. She spent hours helping swimmers improve. The team owes a lot to . . . Lora Davis."

"Lora, you did it!" Tammy screamed. She joined the clapping.

With one strand of hair still in a knot, Lora walked to Mr. Squire. A wide smile creased his face. He handed her a small trophy to keep.

"Thank you," she said.

"No," he told her. "I thank you. Congratulations."

Beaming, Lora danced back to the table. She set the trophy down. It was a small golden statue of a swimmer on a black base. Her mom and dad hugged her. Emily burbled. Lora dropped down on the blanket by Emily. Tammy joined them.

"Your turn next," Lora said.

They looked up at the sound of more clapping. Evan had been chosen Most Inspirational boy. *That's fair,* Tammy thought. Like Lora, he'd spent a lot of time helping the little kids.

"And now," Mr. Squire said, "the 'Most Improved' awards."

Tammy scrunched down. This was the most important moment in her whole life. She'd earned her blue ribbon.

If she got the award, Mr. Squire might ask her to join Firdale. Tammy stared at a dandelion plant at her feet. She couldn't look at him.

"All these kids worked hard," he said, "so these were difficult choices to make. The girl I chose started out with very little swimming experience. She turned out for all the practices, stayed after for extra work. Afternoons, she'd show up and swim laps. Her hard work and talent resulted yesterday in a blue ribbon and triple-A time."

Tammy's mouth was dry. Susan had won a blue ribbon yesterday, too. Had she gotten Triple-A time?

"The winner of this award is . . ." He paused.

Tammy squeezed her eyes shut tight. "Please, please. please," she whispered.

". . . Tammy Tallman."

"Way to go, Tammy," Mayday cried.

Ryan jumped up and down. Lora cheered. Emily burst into tears.

Tammy's chest swelled so she could hardly breathe. Chuck came over and raised her to her feet. Everyone was clapping.

As she walked to Mr. Squire, her smile spread so far it hurt her face. There stood the trophy with her name on it. She touched the letters, felt the roughness of the engraving. It was real.

Mr. Squire handed her the small trophy. "Think about joining Firdale Swim Team next fall," he said.

The balloon in her chest swelled even bigger. "I will, I will," she told him.

She floated back to her table.

"I'm very proud," her mom said, hugging her.

Melissa took the small trophy. "My little sister," she said.

Tammy's excitement turned the rest of the dinner into a blur. She did notice Jim Baxter won Most Improved boy. She cheered the choice of Tom and Mayday for best all-around swimmers. But most of the time, she sat in a daze, holding her trophy. She'd worked so hard to win it. She'd dreamed so often of it. Mr. Squire's words about joining Firdale Swim Team played over and over in her ears. Her mom had to say yes.

Later, at home, Tammy set her trophy on her desk, below the bulletin board and her ribbons. A half-packed suitcase lay open on her bed. The next morning, they would leave for a week's vacation at the ocean. Lora was going, too.

A knock sounded on her door. "Come in," she said.

Chuck entered. He gazed at the trophy. "Looks like it belongs there." He sat in her desk chair. "I spoke with Mr. Squire tonight," he said. "He wants you to join Firdale Swim Team. If your mom agrees, would you like that?"

"Oh, yes," Tammy said. "But will she?"

"Why don't you let me worry about that?"

Tammy studied him. "Why are you doing it?"

"That trophy says it all. You earned this."

Her glance at it brought a quick stab of pleasure. "Thanks, Chuck," she said.

He waved his hand. Standing, he moved to the doorway. "I talked to a doctor the other day, Tammy. He told me if I get allergy shots, I could probably have a kitten around. I might do that this winter." He stepped from the room, closing the door behind him.

For a moment, Tammy stared after him. He'd have shots for her? Shots. Yuk. She winced with the thought.

She crouched by her bed to pull out the kitten's bed she'd made earlier. Patting the towel, she whispered, ''Next spring, Marmalade.''

If you enjoyed following Tammy's
adventures on the summer swim team in
Swim Team #1: Swimmers, Take Your Marks!,
join Lora and Tammy as they face
a new wave of challenges
in this sneak preview of
SWIM TEAM #2: FLY 'N' FREE,
now available from Avon Camelot.

Tammy Tallman gazed at the wide double doors at the end of the hall. They led to the Firdale Swim and Tennis Club's indoor pool. She fiddled with her bathing suit strap.

"Come on, Tammy, we're already late." Grabbing Tammy's hand, Lora Davis, Tammy's best friend, pulled her from the locker room.

"I'm kind of scared," Tammy said.

"Why?" Lora asked. "We just go in and swim with the team. You'll do fine. Don't worry."

Sure, Lora, Tammy thought. *It's easy for you to say. You've been on a year-round swim team before.*

Tammy had signed up for this because Lora wanted her to. Well, that wasn't the only reason. Tammy loved to swim. She just wasn't as good as Lora, or probably the rest of the kids on the team. And that's what really worried her.

"I know something's going to go wrong," Tammy said, "because I dreamed it. I was at this practice. I jumped in the pool, but I couldn't remember how to swim."

"What happened?"

"I sank! The coach pulled me out and told me to go home. Said I was wasting her time."

Lora punched Tammy's arm. "You worry too much! Don't forget, you won the summer team's Most Improved award. You're a good swimmer."

By now, they'd reached the double doors. With her free hand, Lora shoved one open. She towed Tammy through.

Inside, Tammy breathed deeply of the warm, moist air. The smell of chlorine was strong. Before her, the pool stretched almost the length of the room. A divider wide enough to walk on reached across the center. Beyond it, blue ropes of spiral plastic separated the eight lanes.

A group of swimmers around Tammy and Lora's age of eleven stood at that end of the pool. Tammy recognized two of the girls. Hannah and Carrie were their names. And one boy named Jack. They'd swum in the summer league, too.

At that moment, Gail, the coach, came from the office at the end of the pool. "Good to see you all here so early," she said, smiling.

Tammy's eyes went to the wall clock. Six o'clock. The sun hadn't even risen when Tammy left home that morning.

Gail placed a hand on Lora and Tammy's shoulders. "New members. Lora Davis, Tammy Tallman. Mr.

Squire coached them on a summer team. Lora swam for another team before she moved to Seattle. And I'm sure Tammy will fit right in, too. We're lucky to have them."

Everyone was staring at them. Tammy's face warmed. All these kids had been swimming for years. Could they tell she was just a beginner? Lora's hand squeezed hers. She squeezed back.

Gail clapped twice. "Enough chatter. Into the pool for warm-up. Twelve laps."

Water sprayed as everyone jumped in. Tammy pulled her swim cap on. She teetered at the pool edge, her dream at the back of her mind. Lora, already in the pool, grabbed Tammy's foot and pulled her in.

Water fountained around her. She bobbed up and down, getting used to its coolness. Finally, she lay back and kicked. She hadn't sunk! It *had* been just a dream.

She swam twelve laps of freestyle, the stroke she did best. Before last summer, she had called it the crawl stroke. Finishing, she joined Lora and the others at the end of the pool.

"Since it's your first day back, I won't work you too hard," Gail said. "We'll start with six laps of free, in waves. Remember, keep to the right."

She called eight names, including Lora's and Hannah's. The eight lined up with the lanes. The fastest went first. Tammy had learned that during the summer, too.

Gail blew her whistle, and the swimmers dove in. Eight more names, eight more swimmers including Carrie and Jack. Gail called Tammy's name for the third and slowest wave. A short plump girl stood at the lane beside her.

‘‘Hi,’’ the girl said, just as the whistle blew.

Tammy smiled quickly and dove in. She concentrated on moving her arms, flutter kicking, and breathing in the right rhythm. Mr. Squire said she had all the parts right. Now, she had to get them to work together. She wanted Gail to see that she knew what to do.

On the third lap, almost to the wall, she caught up with the second-wave swimmer. She tapped his foot to signal she wanted to pass. He moved out, blocking her way. She didn’t want to slow down. Gail would think she couldn’t handle six laps.

She did an early turn and started her fourth lap ahead of him. Behind her, the water churned. She swam faster to stay ahead. Her next turn was slow. As she came to the surface, a hand grabbed her foot and pulled her back under.

She struggled to get free. He released her and splashed past. She gulped water, coughed and sucked in more. She couldn’t get her breath. She thrashed her arms, trying to stay on top of the water.

Strong hands grabbed her, pulled her from the pool, and pounded her back. Panting, she gazed up at Gail.

‘‘Don’t send me home,’’ Tammy wheezed. Her throat hurt from coughing.

‘‘What went wrong?’’ Gail asked.

A dark-haired boy’s head appeared at pool edge. His hazel eyes drilled into Tammy. *Must have been him,* she thought. She’d like to hold him under for a while, let him see how it felt. But she wouldn’t say anything. She didn’t want these kids to think she was a tattletale.

‘‘Breathed wrong, I guess,’’ she said, blinking back

embarrassed tears. Her first day, and she'd almost drowned, like a baby.

She glanced around, hoping no one had noticed. Hannah and Carrie were talking together. None of the other kids seemed to be paying any attention.

"You were doing fine," Gail went on.

Tammy smiled at the compliment.

"Tammy, what's the matter?"

Tammy turned to Lora's voice. "My dream almost came true."

Lora's eyes widened.

"You were first to finish, Lora," Gail said. "Great job!"

Tammy's pleasure dimmed. She was fine. Lora was great.

Gail clapped her hands. "Everybody, two laps of backstroke!"

Tammy lined up for the next set.

When the hour-long practice was over, Tammy and Lora hurried with the team to the locker room. Everyone rushed to get ready for school. Some took time to call out "Hi, Tammy" and "Hi, Lora. Welcome to the team." Hannah stopped them briefly to say she was glad they'd joined. The plump girl came toward the two as they headed to the showers. Before she said anything, a second girl shoved in front of her. Tammy had seen her swimming in the first wave.

"Hi," she said. "My name's Andrea Conner."